25p

A·L[illegible]E

BY JE[illegible]ER

D0635357

and 15 other stories by famous authors

Deborah Moggach
Richard Adams
Bill James
Anna Reynolds
Antonia Fraser
Doris Lessing
H. R. F. Keating
William Trevor
G. Mackay Brown
Angela Keys
Isabel Colegate
Maeve Binchy
Julian Symons
Hilary Norman
Ruth Rendell

First published in Great Britain in 1995 by Chancellor Press
an imprint of Reed Consumer Books Limited
Michelin House, 81 Fulham Road, London SW3 6RB
and Auckland, Melbourne, Singapore and Toronto

This collection has been compiled and edited by Jason Cheriton

ISBN 1 85152 891 1

Printed in Great Britain
by Cox & Wyman Ltd

Contents

KENSINGTON PALACE

As Patron of the National AIDS Trust, I have often been told by people with HIV and AIDS that one of their worst experiences is the feeling of loneliness - of rejection by society. This anthology of short stories by famous authors who have freely given their talents therefore has a double function. In the first place, it will provide money for the Trust to benefit those affected by the disease, especially the children who may have been born with it. In the second place, it will remind sufferers, as they see the list of familiar names, that they are *not* alone or rejected and that many of the outstanding people of our time care about them. Finally, as well as providing an opportunity for us to show care, the book will undoubtedly give several days enjoyable reading and re-reading. I am delighted to commend this book.

Diana

March, 1995

Introduction

Short stories are a nightmare for the Editor of any magazine which has a reputation for printing them. When I arrived as Editor of the *Literary Review* in Beak Street, the magazine was receiving about a hundredweight of them every month through the post. If the tiny staff had even started to read them, we would have had no time to do anything else, and most of them were drivel. It would be easy to conclude that more people wish to write short stories than wish to read them.

But such a conclusion would be wrong. There is a market for well-written short stories – not a mass market, but a perfectly respectable one, and many people enjoy reading them more than novels. The problem is that the publishing trade nowadays tends to concentrate on trying to produce a few best-sellers. It is not so interested – whether as a result of economic necessity, as it claims, or laziness, as I believe – in earning an honest living from the production of good books which cause much pleasure and selling a couple of thousand copies. The result of this, coupled with magazines' reluctance to touch a medium which has so much unpublishable rubbish waiting to descend on them, is that excellent stories by famous writers, written in a moment of enthusiasm, tend to be put in the author's bottom drawer and forgotten.

Few people write enough short stories to make a book of their own. The result is an anthologist's dream. Jason Cheriton has cracked the system brilliantly. By asking famous writers to offer their work to charity, he successfully bypasses the vanity of so many authors who feel they should be paid enormous sums for their work.

He appeals to them in the most honest and admirable way, to their sense of decency. Finally, by intelligent selection, he has assembled an admirable collection of stories by interesting and important writers. I hope the book raises as much money as possible for the AIDS charity he has in mind and points the way to a successful career for him in the future.

Auberon Waugh

The Inspiration

In September 1989 I met an extraordinarily brave lady whom I shall call Tanya. She looked like an 'ordinary' woman. Although shy at first, Tanya revealed a warm and sensitive disposition. She had, however, been recently widowed. Her husband had died from AIDS at the age of 32 and had left her, then 28 years old, HIV serapositive.

The remarkable thing about Tanya was her vitality and unending desire to help others understand the dire consequences of contracting the HIV infection. The national media gave her plight full attention and I'm sure many people have been encouraged by her stoic bravery. This anthology has been inspired partly as a result of the brief friendship that Tanya and I shared.

I then worked for twelve months on a project which resulted in a charity auction of donated gifts from well-known people for a 'local' AIDS group. To say I was disappointed at the interest shown by the minimal attendance is an understatement – I was angry and vowed to work on another project which *would* be a success.

You have in your hand the result of that promise and I thank you for buying it.

Acknowledgements
My thanks go to Sir John Gielgud, whose generous cheques supplied the means to start this project. Thanks also to Richard Adams, whose story was the first to arrive in late January 1991. This gave me a fine start and the strong incentive needed to see this project through.

Thanks to Ruth Rendell, Deborah Moggach and Lord Jeffrey Archer for taking my phone calls, answering my letters and giving me advice and encouragement, and, of course, thanks to all those authors who said 'yes'. Last, but by no means least, a warm thank you to David and Jane Cornwell for their very generous cheque.

Jason Cheriton

A LA CARTE

Jeffrey Archer

Arthur Hapgood was demobbed on November 3rd, 1946. Within a month he was back at his old workplace on the shop-floor of the Triumph factory on the outskirts of Coventry.

The five years spent in the Sherwood Foresters, four of them as a quartermaster seconded to a tank regiment, only underlined Arthur's likely post-war fate, despite having hoped to find more rewarding work once the war was over. However, on returning to England he quickly discovered that in a 'land fit for heroes' jobs were not that easy to come by, and although he did not want to go back to the work he had done for five years before war had been declared, that of fitting wheels on cars, he reluctantly, after four weeks on the dole, went to see his former works' manager at Triumph.

'The job's yours if you want it, Arthur,' the works' manager assured him.

'And the future?'

'The car's no longer a toy for the eccentric rich or even just a necessity for the businessman,' the works' manager replied. 'In fact,' he continued, 'management are preparing for the "two-car family".'

'So they'll need even more wheels to be put on cars,' said Arthur forlornly.

'That's the ticket.'

Arthur signed on within the hour and it was only a matter of days before he was back into his old routine.

After all, he reminded his wife, it didn't take a degree in engineering to screw four knobs on to a wheel a hundred times a shift.

Arthur soon accepted the fact that he would have to settle for second best. However, second best was not what he planned for his son.

Mark had celebrated his fifth birthday before his father had even set eyes on him, but from the moment Arthur returned home he lavished everything he could on the boy.

Arthur was determined that Mark was not going to end up working on the shop-floor of a car factory for the rest of his life. He put in hours of overtime to earn enough money to ensure that the boy could have extra tuition in maths, general science and English. He felt well rewarded when the boy passed his eleven-plus and won a place at King Henry VIII Grammar School, and that pride did not falter when Mark went on to pass five O-levels and two years later added two A-levels.

Arthur tried not to show his disappointment when, on Mark's eighteenth birthday, the boy informed him that he did not want to go to university.

'What kind of career *are* you hoping to take up then, lad?' Arthur enquired.

'I've filled in an application form to join you on the shop-floor just as soon as I leave school.'

'But why would you —'

'Why not? Most of my friends who're leaving this term have already been accepted by Triumph, and they can't wait to get started.'

'You must be out of your mind.'

'Come off it, Dad. The pay's good and you've shown that there's always plenty of extra money to be picked up with overtime. And I don't mind hard work.'

'Do you think I spent all those years making sure you got a first-class education just to let you end up like me, putting wheels on cars for the rest of your life?' Arthur shouted.

'That's not the whole job and you know it, Dad.'

'You go there over my dead body,' said his father. 'I don't care what your friends end up doing, I only care about you. You could be a solicitor, an accountant, an army officer, even a schoolmaster. Why should you want to end up at a car factory?'

'It's better paid than schoolmastering for a start,' said Mark. 'My French master once told me that he wasn't as well off as you.'

'That's not the point, lad —'

'The point is, Dad, I can't be expected to spend the rest of my life doing a job I don't enjoy just to satisfy one of your fantasies.'

'Well, I'm not going to allow you to waste the rest of your life,' said Arthur, getting up from the breakfast table. 'The first thing I'm going to do when I get in to work this morning is see that your application is turned down.'

'That isn't fair, Dad. I have the right to —'

But his father had already left the room, and did not utter another word to the boy before leaving for the factory.

For over a week father and son didn't speak to each other. It was Mark's mother who was left to come up with the compromise. Mark could apply for any job that met with his father's approval and as long as he completed a year at that job he could, if he still wanted to, reapply to work at the factory. His father for his part would not then put any obstacle in his son's way.

Arthur nodded. Mark also reluctantly agreed to the solution.

'But only if you complete the full year,' Arthur warned solemnly.

During those last days of the summer holiday Arthur came up with several suggestions for Mark to consider, but the boy showed no enthusiasm for any of them. Mark's mother became quite anxious that her son would end up with no job at all until, while helping her slice potatoes for dinner one night, Mark confided that he thought hotel management seemed the least unattractive proposition he had considered so far.

'At least you'd have a roof over your head and be regularly fed,' his mother said.

'Bet they don't cook as well as you, Mum,' said Mark as

he placed the sliced potatoes on the top of the Lancashire hot-pot. 'Still, it's only a year.'

During the next month Mark attended several interviews at hotels around the country without success. It was then that his father discovered that his old company sergeant was head porter at the Savoy: immediately Arthur started to pull a few strings.

'If the boy's any good,' Arthur's old comrade-in-arms assured him over a pint, 'he could end up as a head porter, even a hotel manager.' Arthur seemed well satisfied, even though Mark was still assuring his friends that he would be joining them a year to the day.

On September 1st, 1959, Arthur and Mark Hapgood travelled together by bus to Coventry station. Arthur shook hands with the boy and promised him, 'Your mother and I will make sure it's a special Christmas this year when they give you your first leave. And don't worry – you'll be in good hands with "Sarge". He'll teach you a thing or two. Just remember to keep your nose clean.'

Mark said nothing and returned a thin smile as he boarded the train. 'You'll never regret it . . .' were the last words Mark heard his father say as the train pulled out of the station.

Mark regretted it from the moment he set foot in the hotel.

As a junior porter he started his day at six in the morning and ended at six in the evening. He was entitled to a fifteen-minute mid-morning break, a forty-five-minute lunch break and another fifteen-minute break around mid-afternoon. After the first month had passed he could not recall when he had been granted all three breaks on the same day, and he quickly learned that there was no one to whom he could protest. His duties consisted of carrying guests' cases up to their rooms, then lugging them back down again the moment they wanted to leave. With an average of three hundred people staying in the hotel each night the process was endless. The pay turned out to be half what his friends were getting back home and as he had to hand over all his tips to the head porter, however much overtime Mark put in, he never saw an extra penny. On the only occasion he dared to mention it to the head porter he was met with the words, 'Your time will come, lad.'

It did not worry Mark that his uniform didn't fit or that his room was six foot by six foot and overlooked Charing Cross Station, or even that he didn't get a share of the tips; but it did worry him that there was nothing he could do to please the head porter – however clean he kept his nose.

Sergeant Crann, who considered the Savoy nothing more than an extension of his old platoon, didn't have a lot of time for young men under his command who hadn't done their national service.

'But I wasn't *eligible* to do national service,' insisted Mark. 'No one born after 1939 was called up.'

'Don't make excuses, lad.'

'It's not an excuse, Sarge. It's the truth.'

'And don't call me "Sarge". I'm "Sergeant Crann" to you, and don't you forget it.'

'Yes, Sergeant Crann.'

At the end of each day Mark would return to his little box-room with its small bed, small chair and tiny chest of drawers, and collapse exhausted. The only picture in the room – of the Laughing Cavalier – was on the calendar that hung above Mark's bed. The date of September 1st, 1960, was circled in red to remind him when he would be allowed to re-join his friends at the factory back home. Each night before falling asleep he would cross out the offending day like a prisoner making scratch marks on a wall.

At Christmas Mark returned home for a four-day break, and when his mother saw the general state of the boy she tried to talk his father into allowing Mark to give up the job early, but Arthur remained implacable.

'We made an agreement. I can't be expected to get him a job at the factory if he isn't responsible enough to keep to his part of a bargain.'

During the holiday Mark waited for his friends outside the factory gate until their shift had ended and listened to their stories of weekends spent watching football, drinking at the pub and dancing to the Everly Brothers.

They all sympathised with his problem and looked forward to him joining them in September. 'It's only a few more months,' one of them reminded him cheerfully.

Far too quickly, Mark was on the journey back to London, where he continued unwillingly to hump cases up and down the hotel corridors for month after month.

Once the English rain had subsided the usual influx of American tourists began. Mark liked the Americans, who treated him as an equal and often tipped him a shilling when others would have given him only sixpence. But whatever the amount Mark received Sergeant Crann would still pocket it with the inevitable, 'Your time will come, lad.'

One such American for whom Mark ran around diligently every day during his fortnight's stay ended up presenting the boy with a ten-bob note as he left the front entrance of the hotel.

Mark said, 'Thank you, sir,' and turned round to see Sergeant Crann standing in his path.

'Hand it over,' said Crann as soon as the American visitor was well out of earshot.

'I was going to the moment I saw you,' said Mark, passing the note to his superior.

'Not thinking of pocketing what's rightfully mine, was you?'

'No, I wasn't,' said Mark. 'Though God knows I earned it.'

'Your time will come, lad,' said Sergeant Crann without much thought.

'Not while someone as mean as you is in charge,' replied Mark sharply.

'What was that you said?' asked the head porter, veering round.

'You heard me the first time, Sarge.'

The clip across the ear took Mark by surprise.

'You, lad, have just lost your job. Nobody, but nobody, talks to me like that.' Sergeant Crann turned and set off smartly in the direction of the manager's office.

The hotel manager, Gerald Drummond, listened to the head porter's version of events before asking Mark to report to his office immediately. 'You realise I have been left with no choice but to sack you,' were his first words once the door was closed.

Mark looked up at the tall, elegant man in his long, black coat, white collar and black tie. 'Am I allowed to tell you what actually happened, sir?' he asked.

Mr Drummond nodded, then listened without interruption as Mark gave his version of what had taken place that morning, and also disclosed the agreement he had entered into with his father. 'Please let me complete my final ten weeks,' Mark ended, 'or my father will only say I haven't kept my end of our bargain.'

'I haven't got another job vacant at the moment,' protested the manager. 'Unless you're willing to peel potatoes for ten weeks.'

'Anything,' said Mark.

'Then report to the kitchen at six tomorrow morning. I'll tell the third chef to expect you. Only if you think the head porter is a martinet just wait until you meet Jacques, our *maître chef de cuisine*. He won't clip your ear, he'll cut it off.'

Mark didn't care. He felt confident that for just ten weeks he could face anything, and at five thirty the following morning he exchanged his dark blue uniform for a white top and blue and white check trousers before reporting for his new duties. To his surprise the kitchen took up almost the entire basement of the hotel, and was even more of a bustle than the lobby had been.

The third chef put him in the corner of the kitchen, next to a mountain of potatoes, a bowl of cold water and a sharp knife. Mark peeled through breakfast, lunch and dinner, and fell asleep on his bed that night without even enough energy left to cross a day off his calendar.

For the first week he never actually saw the fabled Jacques. With seventy people working in the kitchens Mark felt confident he could pass his whole period there without anyone being aware of him.

Each morning at six he would start peeling, then hand over the potatoes to a gangling youth called Terry who in turn would dice or cut them according to the third chef's instructions for the dish of the day. Monday sauté, Tuesday mashed, Wednesday French-fried, Thursday sliced,

Friday roast, Saturday croquette . . . Mark quickly worked out a routine which kept him well ahead of Terry and therefore out of any trouble.

Having watched Terry do his job for over a week Mark felt sure he could have shown the young apprentice how to lighten his workload quite simply, but he decided to keep his mouth closed: opening it might only get him into more trouble, and he was certain the manager wouldn't give him a second chance.

Mark soon discovered that Terry always fell badly behind on Tuesday's shepherd's pie and Thursday's Lancashire hot-pot. From time to time the third chef would come across to complain and he would glance over at Mark to be sure that it wasn't him who was holding the process up. Mark made certain that he always had a spare tub of peeled potatoes by his side so that he escaped censure.

It was on the first Thursday morning in August (Lancashire hot-pot) that Terry sliced off the top of his forefinger. Blood spurted all over the sliced potatoes and on to the wooden table as the lad began yelling hysterically.

'Get him out of here!' Mark heard the *maître chef de cuisine* bellow above the noise of the kitchen as he stormed towards them.

'And you,' he said, pointing at Mark, 'clean up mess and start slicing rest of potatoes. I 'ave eight hundred hungry customers still expecting to feed.'

'Me?' said Mark in disbelief. 'But —'

'Yes, you. You couldn't do worse job than idiot who calls himself trainee chef and cuts off finger.' The chef marched away, leaving Mark to move reluctantly across to the table where Terry had been working. He felt disinclined to argue while the calendar was there to remind him that he was down to his last twenty-five days.

Mark set about a task he had carried out for his mother many times. The clean, neat cuts were delivered with a skill Terry would never learn to master. By the end of the day, although exhausted, Mark did not feel quite as tired as he had in the past.

At eleven that night the *maître chef de cuisine* threw off

his hat and barged out of the swing doors, a sign to everyone else they could also leave the kitchen once everything that was their responsibility had been cleared up. A few seconds later the door swung back open and the chef burst in. He stared round the kitchen as everyone waited to see what he would do next. Having found what he was looking for, he headed straight for Mark.

'Oh, my God,' thought Mark. 'He's going to kill me.'

'How is your name?' the chef demanded.

'Mark Hapgood, sir,' he managed to splutter out.

'You waste on 'tatoes, Mark Hapgood,' said the chef. 'You start on vegetables in morning. Report at seven. If that *crétin* with half finger ever returns, put him to peeling 'tatoes.'

The chef turned on his heel even before Mark had the chance to reply. He dreaded the thought of having to spend three weeks in the middle of the kitchens, never once out of the *maître chef de cuisine*'s sight, but he accepted there was no alternative.

The next morning Mark arrived at six for fear of being late and spent an hour watching the fresh vegetables being unloaded from Covent Garden market. The hotel's supply manager checked every case carefully, rejecting several before he signed a chit to show the hotel had received over three thousand pounds' worth of vegetables. An average day, he assured Mark.

The *maître chef de cuisine* appeared a few minutes before seven thirty, checked the menus and told Mark to score the Brussels sprouts, trim the French beans and remove the coarse outer leaves of the cabbages.

'But I don't know how,' Mark replied honestly. He could feel the other trainees in the kitchen edging away from him.

'Then I teach you,' roared the chef. 'Perhaps only thing you learn is if hope to be good chef, you able to do everyone's job in kitchen, even 'tato peeler's.

'But I'm hoping to be a . . .' Mark began and then thought better of it. The chef seemed not to have heard Mark as he took his place beside the new recruit. Everyone in the kitchen stared as the chef began to show Mark the basic skills of cutting, dicing and slicing.

'And remember other idiot's finger,' the chef said on completing the lesson and passing the razor-sharp knife back to Mark. 'Yours can be next.'

Mark started gingerly dicing the carrots, then the Brussels sprouts, removing the outer layer before cutting a firm cross in the stalk. Next he moved on to trimming and slicing the beans. Once again he found it fairly easy to keep ahead of the chef's requirements.

At the end of each day, after the head chef had left, Mark stayed on to sharpen all his knives in preparation for the following morning, and would not leave his work area until it was spotless.

On the sixth day, after a curt nod from the chef, Mark realised he must be doing something half-right. By the following Saturday he felt he had mastered the simple skills of vegetable preparation and found himself becoming fascinated by what the chef himself was up to. Although Jacques rarely addressed anyone as he marched round the acre of kitchen except to grunt his approval or disapproval – the latter more commonly – Mark quickly learned to anticipate his needs. Within a short space of time he began to feel that he was part of a team – even though he was only too aware of being the novice recruit.

On the deputy chef's day off the following week Mark was allowed to arrange the cooked vegetables in their bowls and spent some time making each dish look attractive as well as edible. The chef not only noticed but actually muttered his greatest accolade – '*Bon*.'

During his last three weeks at the Savoy Mark did not even look at the calendar above his bed.

One Thursday morning a message came down from the under-manager that Mark was to report to his office as soon as was convenient. Mark had quite forgotten that it was August 31st – his last day. He cut ten lemons into quarters, then finished preparing the forty plates of thinly sliced smoked salmon that would complete the first course for a wedding lunch. He looked with pride at his efforts before folding up his apron and leaving to collect his papers and final wage packet.

'Where you think you're going?' asked the chef, looking up.

'I'm off,' said Mark. 'Back to Coventry.'

'See you Monday then. You deserve day off.'

'No, I'm going home for good,' said Mark.

The chef stopped checking the cuts of rare beef that would make up the second course of the wedding feast.

'Going?' he repeated as if he didn't understand the word.

'Yes. I've finished my year and now I'm off home to work.'

'I hope you found first-class hotel,' said the chef with genuine interest.

'I'm not going to work in a hotel.'

'A restaurant, perhaps?'

'No, I'm going to get a job at Triumph.'

The chef looked puzzled for a moment, unsure if it was his English or whether the boy was mocking him.

'What is – Triumph?'

'A place where they manufacture cars.'

'You will manufacture cars?'

'Not a whole car, but I will put the wheels on.'

'You put cars on wheels?' the chef said in disbelief.

'No,' laughed Mark. 'Wheels on cars.'

The chef still looked uncertain.

'So you will be cooking for car workers?'

'No. As I explained, I'm going to put the wheels on the cars,' said Mark slowly, enunciating each word.

'That not possible.'

'Oh yes it is,' responded Mark. 'And I've waited a whole year to prove it.'

'If I offered you job as commis chef, you change mind?' asked the chef quietly.

'Why would you do that?'

'Because you 'ave talent in those fingers. In time I think you become chef, perhaps even good chef.'

'No, thanks. I'm off to Coventry to join my mates.'

The head chef shrugged. '*Tant pis*,' he said, and without a second glance returned to the carcass of beef. He glanced over at the plates of smoked salmon. 'A wasted talent,' he added after the swing door had closed behind his potential protégé.

Mark locked his room, threw the calendar in the waste-paper basket and returned to the hotel to hand in his kitchen clothes to the housekeeper. The final action he took was to return his room key to the under-manager.

'Your wage packet, your cards and your PAYE. Oh, and the chef has phoned up to say he would be happy to give you a reference,' said the under-manager. 'Can't pretend that happens every day.'

'Won't need that where I'm going,' said Mark. 'But thanks all the same.'

He started off for the station at a brisk pace, his small battered suitcase swinging by his side, only to find that each step took a little longer. When he arrived at Euston he made his way to Platform 7 and began walking up and down, occasionally staring at the great clock above the booking hall. He watched first one train and then another pull out of the station bound for Coventry. He was aware of the station becoming dark as shadows filtered through the glass awning on to the public concourse. Suddenly he turned and walked off at an even brisker pace. If he hurried he could still be back in time to help chef prepare dinner that night.

Mark trained under Jacques le Renneu for five years. Vegetables were followed by sauces, fish by poultry, meats by pâtisserie. After eight years at the Savoy he was appointed second chef, and had learned so much from his mentor that regular patrons could no longer be sure when it was the *maître chef de cuisine*'s day off. Two years later Mark became a master chef, and when in 1971 Jacques was offered the opportunity to return to Paris and take over the kitchens of the George Cinq – an establishment that is to Paris what Harrods is to London – Jacques agreed, but only on condition that Mark accompanied him.

'It is wrong direction from Coventry,' Jacques warned him, 'and in any case they sure to offer you my job at the Savoy.'

'I'd better come along otherwise those Frogs will never get a decent meal.'

'Those Frogs,' said Jacques, 'will always know when it's my day off.'

'Yes, and book in even greater numbers,' suggested Mark, laughing.

It was not to be long before Parisians were flocking to the George Cinq, not to rest their weary heads but to relish the cooking of the two-chef team.

When Jacques celebrated his sixty-fifth birthday the great hotel did not have to look far to appoint his successor.

'The first Englishman ever to be *maître chef de cuisine* at the George Cinq,' said Jacques, raising a glass of champagne at his farewell banquet. 'Who would believe it? Of course, you will have to change your name to Marc to hold down such a position.'

'Neither will ever happen,' said Mark.

'Oh yes it will, because I 'ave recommended you.'

'Then I shall turn it down.'

'Going to put cars on wheels, *peut-être*?' asked Jacques mockingly.

'No, but I have found a little restaurant on the Left Bank. With my savings alone I can't quite afford the lease, but with your help . . .'

Chez Jacques opened on the rue du Plaisir on the Left Bank on May 1st, 1982, and it was not long before those customers who had taken the George Cinq for granted transferred their allegiance.

Mark's reputation spread as the two chefs pioneered 'nouvelle cuisine', and soon the only way anyone could be guaranteed a table at the restaurant in under three weeks was to be a film star or a Cabinet Minister.

The day Michelin gave Chez Jacques their third star Mark, with Jacques's blessing, decided to open a second restaurant. The press and customers then quarrelled amongst themselves as to which was the finer establishment. The booking sheets showed clearly the public felt there was no difference.

When in October 1986 Jacques died, at the age of seventy-one, the restaurant critics wrote confidently that standards were bound to fall. A year later the same journalists had to admit that one of the five great chefs of France had come from a town in the British Midlands they could not even pronounce.

Jacques's death only made Mark yearn more for his homeland, and when he read in the *Daily Telegraph* of a new development to be built in Covent Garden he called the site agent to ask for more details.

Mark's third restaurant was opened in the heart of London on February 11th, 1987.

Over the years Mark Hapgood often travelled back to Coventry to see his parents. His father had retired long since but Mark was still unable to persuade either parent to take the trip to Paris and sample his culinary efforts. But now he had opened in the country's capital he hoped to tempt them.

'We don't need to go up to London,' said his mother, laying the table. 'You always cook for us whenever you come home, and we read of your successes in the papers. In any case, your father isn't so good on his legs nowadays.'

'What do you call this, son?' his father asked a few minutes later as noisette of lamb surrounded by baby carrots was placed in front of him.

'Nouvelle cuisine.'

'And people pay good money for it?'

Mark laughed and the following day prepared his father's favourite Lancashire hot-pot.

'Now that's a real meal,' said Arthur after his third helping. 'And I'll tell you something for nothing, lad. You cook it almost as well as your mother.'

A year later Michelin announced the restaurants throughout the world that had been awarded their coveted third star. *The Times* let its readers know on its front page that Chez Jacques was the first English restaurant ever to be so honoured.

To celebrate the award Mark's parents finally agreed to make the journey down to London, though not until Mark had sent a telegram saying he was reconsidering that job at British Leyland. He sent a car to fetch his parents and had them installed in a suite at the Savoy. That evening he reserved the most popular table at Chez Jacques in their name.

Vegetable soup followed by steak and kidney pie with a

plate of bread and butter pudding to end on were not the table d'hôte that night, but they were served for the special guests on Table 17.

Under the influence of the finest wine, Arthur was soon chatting happily to anyone who would listen and couldn't resist reminding the head waiter that it was his son who owned the restaurant.

'Don't be silly, Arthur,' said his wife. 'He already knows that.'

'Nice couple, your parents,' the head waiter confided to his boss after he had served them with their coffee and supplied Arthur with a cigar. 'What did your old man do before he retired? Banker, lawyer, schoolmaster?'

'Oh no, nothing like that,' said Mark quietly. 'He spent the whole of his working life putting wheels on cars.'

'But why would he waste his time doing that?' asked the waiter incredulously.

'Because he wasn't lucky enough to have a father like mine,' Mark replied.

LUCKY DIP

Deborah Moggach

The point of raffles is that you never win. You don't expect to, do you? It's like The Pools; it happens to somebody else.

In fact, by the end of the evening I'd forgotten I had even bought a ticket. This happened last January, at a Firestone Tyres dinner. I had gone with a mate of mine, also in the motor trade. His girlfriend had tonsilitis, so he had asked me to go instead and I thought: why not? During cocktails I had bought a ticket, they practically forced you. It was on behalf of something worthy – Distressed Morgan-Owners, or the Old Alvis Sanctuary, I didn't really hear. I had forgotten all about the ticket, in the pocket of my hired DJ. When they read the number out it sounded unfamiliar, like a bus route you don't take, and then – thump – I suddenly realised it was mine. First Prize.

I had to walk up to the platform and meet an actress. You might have recognised her; she plays a vet's assistant, on afternoon TV. People started clapping and she gave me my envelope. Just for a moment, the room echoed and the faces shrank. Fame at last. It was a holiday for two in Portugal.

Chance. A hand gropes in a hat, the fingers touch a scrap of paper. I run a garage, you see – Paradise Motors. It's in Paradise Mews, Cricklewood, hence the name. Victims of chance are our stock-in-trade. A chance collision, metal against metal, the crunch of two innocent little errands and bang. Usually I'm too busy to realise the randomness of it all, but sometimes I straighten up, oily and awe-struck.

So an actress had groped in a hat and given me a week in the Algarve. Trouble was, the two.

Now, a romantic holiday in Portugal is just the ticket if you've got somebody to be romantic with. Since my divorce I'd had one or two girlfriends but the whole thing had been vaguely unsatisfactory, probably due to me. I had been humiliated and, like a car-crash, if you've had one you drive more carefully for a while. Just slipping into the front seat, you're aware of the possibilities. This makes for a tentative expedition.

I couldn't call them up again. 'Remember me – Graham? How about a rekindling week at the Marichoro Apartments, courtesy of Sunspan Holidays?' I didn't even know their phone numbers unless I rang their parents, and I only knew one lot of those. The whole idea was pathetic. So was taking my sister, who was a chiropodist in Finchley and longing for a jaunt. Blokes were out, needless to say. I'd never live it down.

Two dates were offered for this holiday – March and November. For the first few months I refused to panic. There was plenty of time. It seemed so far away that I was actually looking forward to it. Didn't I deserve a break? Something, someone, somehow, would turn up.

March came and went, blustery and cold. April, May, and then June, blustery and somehow colder. By August I was starting to get anxious.

I couldn't confide in Norm. He's the bloke I work with, and he's been married for thirty-three years. Besides, his wife's got a hip and he spends his lunch-breaks doing the shopping. He's very nice, but not the responsive type; in fact he collects tropical fish. He thinks I'm an intellectual because I read Dick Francis.

Then there was Reg. He's in the next premises and he does our panel-beating. Single-handed, he's kept the property prices down in this locality; in fact, with a brisk west wind you can hear him in Swiss Cottage. Reg's office is wallpapered with wet T-shirt calendars from sparking plug firms. He wasn't the ideal person for a delicate conversation of this nature.

I couldn't possibly go on holiday by myself; not when it was a prize. They would be expecting a loving couple; the manager would greet us with a wink and bowl of fruit. I had been away alone, of course, but only to lowly-sexed locations like the Lake District. Portugal was sun and sand and sangria. I have been to Spain, you see.

As the months dragged on I even considered, for a mad moment, giving it a miss altogether. There was a beauty club I had passed in the Tufnell Park Road, when I went to tow away a Toyota. It offered sun beds. I could take a week off and return to Paradise Motors mahogany and smug. I could play it mysterious and keep Reg on tenterhooks.

However, there was my own self-esteem to think of. I did have some left. By this time I had forgotten that the whole thing was supposed to be pleasant. By now it was just something to be got through, willy-nilly. To tell the truth, by now anyone would do.

Female customers were another possibility. The trouble with them was my invisibility. To most of them I was just some geezer in greasy overalls who presented them with a bill for about twice as much as they expected, because garage bills always are.

There were some I liked, of course. There was one girl with a temperamental Metro – a contradiction in terms, with a Metro, but you hadn't seen her clutch-abuse. She actually knew my name, Graham, and we'd had some interesting conversations about Alfred Hitchcock because she was a film buff. Then there was a saucy type in a 2CV, the lentil-eater's car. Unlike our other 2CV customers, however, she wore short skirts and had a terrific pair of legs. But how could I manage the jump from 'It's passed its MOT' to 'What about a holiday for two in Portugal?'

Anyway, they were mostly married. It was Postman Pat cassettes all over the floor and Mrs on their cheques. The only other possibility was a Ms Hodges, who drove an Escort XR3. But she had a carphone, which I somehow found deflating. I know most men wouldn't, but there you go.

Still, attraction was no longer my first priority. Not even a consideration, really. Anybody reasonably able-bodied, female gender, under sixty, would do. By the end of August Reg was getting leery. 'Go on. Give us a butchers, you sly bugger.'

And then, on August 21, Sharon came in with her Capri. It was a flash job – 2.8, alloy wheels, spoilers, two tone champagne/silver, the works. She had pranged its bonnet.

'They shouldn't have made it a one-way street' she said irritably.

I though it was a surprising car for her to drive, but you get some funny matches, with motors. Like marriage, really.

She dropped in the next day, on the off-chance it was ready (it wasn't).

'I only work up the road,' she said. 'At Hair Today. It's no trouble.'

I was under the hood of a Cavalier, wrestling with a brake pad. I came out and wiped my hands.

'Fancy a lager?' I asked. Suddenly summer had started, and I was sweltering.

She nodded. It was lunchtime, and Norm had gone off to buy some pond weed. We sat down on a couple of oil drums. After we had opened the Heinekens, a silence fell. It always does just then, doesn't it.

'Been on your holidays yet?' she asked, and then giggled. 'Where I work, it's what you get asked half the year. The other half it's —'

'What are you doing for Christmas?'

She laughed. Like most hairdressers her own hair was a real mess – bleached bits growing out. She was very pretty, and sort of frayed around the edges in a vaguely promising way. Her slingbacks were trodden down at the back and she had a little crucifix around her neck; I remembered from my younger days that this was a good sign.

Luckily I didn't have to answer about the holidays because Reg came over to tell her how much it would cost to knock out the dents in her Capri, and she rolled her eyes.

When she had gone he rolled his. 'Wouldn't mind looking under her bonnet,' he said.

In October she came back again. This time she had dented the back bumper of the car, and crunched the boot.

'I was only putting on my brakes,' she said. 'The silly cow wasn't looking.'

It was raining, so we sat in the office and had a cup of coffee. Today she had re-bleached her hair and it was tied up in a plastic comb. She looked young and ripe.

'So what are you doing for Christmas?' I asked.

She laughed. 'Haven't even had me hols yet. I was going to Yugoslavia with my friend Beverley, but she went off with a married man and I couldn't go alone, could I?'

'I know the feeling,' I said. Then I took a breath. There was a silence, broken by a tattoo of hammer-blows from next door. 'Ever fancied Portugal?'

So off we went, 5 am on a November morning. Gatwick to Faro, with Sharon sitting beside me in a new yellow T-shirt and slacks.

'Is my lipstick straight?' she asked. 'It was so dark when we left.'

As the plane lifted I felt dizzy with the chanciness of it all. If Evelyn hadn't got tonsilitis; if the actress had picked another raffle ticket; if that other car had arrived three seconds later and Sharon hadn't bumped into it . . . My palms were clammy. What on earth were we going to do?

'What are you thinking?' she asked.

I jumped. 'I was just wondering where old bank notes go when they get old. Do they just get dirtier and dirtier and fall to bits, and the last person's the unlucky one?'

She burst out laughing. 'I can see this is going to be a hoot.'

The Manichoro Apartments was a high-rise building surrounded by bulldozers. Skyscrapers were being built all around us; the air was filled with hammering and drilling. It was like a hundred Reg's, out there. We went to our room.

'For the happy couple!' shouted the manager, giving us

our starter pack. This had bread rolls in it, and little packets of instant coffee.

I edged towards the bedroom and peered in. Twin beds.

It was off-season and the place was deserted, except for five or six old dears who were sitting around the pool. They eyes us with interest when we joined them.

'I'm from Melton Mowbray,' said one of them, who had spread her tapestry over three sunloungers. 'But we always come here for the winter, don't we, Dot?'

Out in the street the drilling started. Dot shouted: 'It's nice to see some fresh young faces, isn't it?' She turned to us. 'There's bingo tonight, it's all go, then it's whist tomorrow, and your last night it's Sangria'n'Disco.'

Sharon had stripped down to her bikini, and was anointing herself with Ambre Solaire. She had a lovely body, plumpish but compact.

'Wonder what Vic's going to say,' she murmured, lying back.

'Vic?'

'About the bills for the car. It's his.'

'Who's Vic?' I asked.

'My boyfriend.' She closed her eyes.

Three days passed. We sat beside the pool, and inspected the range of teabags in the supermarket. We played ping-pong in the deserted, concrete games room and had free drinks with timeshare touts. It was about three miles to the sea, through building sites, but at least it was an expedition. One of the places on the beach was open, and it served chips.

The whole business wasn't quite as I had expected, but Sharon didn't seem to mind. She had turned a shy pink, and freckles appeared on her nose. At night, after the evening's entertainments downstairs, we modestly changed into our pyjamas, she in the bedroom and me in the bathroom, and climbed into our twin beds. Then we read our books; luckily I had brought enough for two. Outside in the corridor we heard the clunk-clunk of Ruby's walking frame, as she made her way back from the bar.

On Wednesday night Sharon put down her John Le Carré; she had forgotten which spy was which.

'Tell me about your wife,' she said.

'Ex,' I corrected. 'She worked in the perfumery department at Selfridges, squirting aftershave at strange men. I knew it was a mistake.'

'What happened?'

'One day she scored a direct hit. It turned out to be a sheik and she ran away with him, back to wherever it was, the Yemen, somewhere horrible. I've never known.'

There was a pause. Outside, the drilling had stopped. Sometimes it seemed to go on all night.

'Tell me about Vic,' I said.

'Oh, he's in prison.'

I paused. 'What for?'

'GBH.'

'What's that?'

'Grievous bodily harm.'

'Ah,' I said. 'Of course.'

'Nighty-night.' She switched off her light.

By the next day she was turning a delicious shade of honey. We lay beside the pool. I had graduated to rubbing her with suntan oil.

'Mmm,' she murmured into her towel. 'A bit lower.'

'Have you tried the supermarket opposite Spud'U'Like?' shouted Ruby, above the noise. 'Their *Daily Telegraph*'s only a day late.'

I went on rubbing oil into Sharon's firm, stocky thighs. My mouth was dry with desire. But if it happened, and it wasn't a success, how were we going to get through the next three days? And did she want it, anyway? Above all, what about Vic? I pictured him attacking me, a Reg hammering at my helpless bodywork.

'When's he coming out,' I asked. 'From, you know?'

'Vic? The week after we get back.'

Our last night was Sangria'n'Disco. The Sunspan rep, a jovial heterosexual called Malcolm, filled and refilled our glasses. Afterwards a combo played and we danced the hokey-cokey with Dot and Co. I gripped frail, bony arms and kicked my legs. Then we drank some more and sang that song: 'With a little bit of this' . . . We wiggled our fingers. 'And a little bit of that.'

'And a little bit of the other,' leered Malcolm. 'For the lucky ones.'

Finally there was a slow number. The ladies got out their knitting. To the accompaniment of clicking needles I drew Sharon close, and breathed in the chlorine scent of her hair.

'I want to leave him,' she murmured. 'But you can't, when they're in prison. Anyway, he's got my name tattooed somewhere special, and it's ever so painful to get it removed. Especially there.' We shuffled a few steps. 'How could he get another girlfriend? The name would be wrong.'

That night, inflamed by alcohol, I kissed her, and finally we stumbled into my twin bed.

Afterwards she stroked my cheek. 'Know something?' she said. 'Your wife was daft!'

That was a month ago. It's Christmas now, the season of forgiveness, and for once something like that seems to have happened.

Vic came out of prison a changed man. Apparently they'd had a visiting creative writer, at the Scrubs, and Vic went to see him because it meant skiving laundry rota. He had ended up writing a poem, something about the bird of freedom beating its wings, and it won the Arthur Koestler prize (£200) for something arty done whilst behind bars.

When he came out he was a celebrity, and much in demand at writers' circles where he charmed genteel ladies with his pugilistic good looks. One of the ladies was quite young. She was aiming for Mills and Boon and he must have seemed like a dream come true.

Sharon and I met him at a pub, for a festive drink. His new girlfriend was sitting beside him. She wore glasses and a sort of kaftan thing.

I thought of his tattoo.

'Don't tell me,' I said. 'Let me guess your name.'

She put down her shandy and said coyly: 'Go on then.'

'Sharon.'
She took off her specs, and stared. Then she nodded.
Beside me, from my own Sharon, I heard a giggle.

A DOG IN THE DARK

Richard Adams

No one could possibly call me an imaginative bloke or given to flights of fancy. In fact, I suppose you could hunt all over the country and not find a more completely ordinary bloke than I am. I'm twenty-six and unmarried. I got four O-levels at comprehensive school at Reading and I work as a traveller for Briggs and Murrayson. What do I travel in? Curtain and carpet patterns. They give me a Ford Fiesta hatchback and I cover a round of shops and warehouses across the south and midlands. Well, I mean, people have got to have patterns: it's honest work, and there's prospects of a sort. I'm not all that ambitious, anyway.

I've got nice digs – been there five years now – just outside Basingstoke. There's only two other lodgers. Mrs Forster's a decent old girl and she seems to like me. She sees to my washing and if I get in late she'll nearly always make me a cup of tea and open a tin of pasta or baked beans and sausages. She's a kind soul as long as you're careful not to make a noise or bring mud into the house. And best of all, she positively liked Bruce and never made the least objection to me keeping him.

Bruce was my dog. He was a black-and-white Welsh border collie – you've seen hundreds. Only not like Bruce. He was the best-trained, most obedient, responsive dog you ever could see. I trained him myself: all I did was to buy a book and do what it said, and it worked like a charm: so it just shows how lazy and irresponsible most dog-owners are, doesn't it? By the time he was two, Bruce would come when he was called, sit, lie down, keep completely still while another dog sniffed him over, stop dead in his tracks at a hundred yards and walk to heel. The book says walking to heel's the equivalent of higher education for a dog and not to do too much of it too soon. It says the whole secret is building up a close personal relationship with the dog; and that's what we had, me and Bruce. He used to sleep on my bed and Mrs Forster didn't mind. She was very fond of Bruce. She admired his obedience.

Bruce used to be the big thing in my life. Mind you, I know a few girls, but nothing serious – not yet. Bruce was my creation, but in a funny sort of way I was his creation too. I never did anything without Bruce. Weekends, we used to get in some terrific walks on the Downs: and when I went out on the job in the Fiesta, Bruce always came too, every day. He used to sit in the back, on his own rug. He got to know all the places we went to, and when I stopped at a Little Chef I used to take a snack out to Bruce. Only a snack, though. The book says a dog should have one good meal a day, in the evening, and that's what he got. Some of the clients got to know old Bruce very well. You could say he was good for business – broke the ice, you know.

Well, now, it was a December night about fifteen months ago – winter before last – and I was driving home a bit later than usual, and taking things carefully, because there were patches of fog. I turned on to a minor road near Hartley Wintney, partly because if you know the way it's a short cut and partly because I was busting for a pee. I pulled up in the dark – side-lights left on, of course – where the road runs through a wood, got out, went across to the other side of the road where there were some bushes (I hate peeing against the wheel) and got on with it. I'd left the driver's door open and that's something I'll regret to my dying day. I was in full stream, as you might say, when I saw Bruce jump over the driving seat and push his way out. I expect he wanted a pee, too, and anyway I hadn't told him to stay where he was. He was in the middle of the road, crossing to me, when I heard a car coming and saw its lights.

In the normal way I'd have run over to Bruce, but – well, I mean, I couldn't, could I? I shouted 'Bruce, stop!' And that's where I made my fatal mistake, because he did stop – he stopped right there in the road. At the same moment the car, a grey Peugeot 309 going much too fast, came ripping round the corner – spotlighting me – and knocked Bruce flying onto the verge. There was only one man in it: he didn't stop: didn't even slow down, although he must have felt the impact. In two seconds he was gone and I hadn't got the number. But I'd noticed a discoloured patch on the boot.

Bruce died in my arms about two minutes later. He was trying to lick my face. I'm not ashamed to tell you I was crying my eyes out. Wouldn't you? Never mind how I took him home and disposed of him. Mrs Forster, good old soul, was terribly upset, too. I kept his collar. It's on the dressing-table now.

Things just weren't the same without Bruce. I felt wretchedly lonely. I couldn't bear to walk on the Downs without him. My bed at night didn't feel the same. The long drives all day were miserable. Sometimes I'd wake up in the morning and I'd have forgotten and for a second I felt happy. Then it all came flooding back and I could hardly get up and shave. Mrs Forster was very kind and motherly, but I mean, what could she do? I thought of getting another dog, but it didn't appeal – didn't seem decent to replace Bruce like a pen or a pair of shoes. I drove alone. Sometimes I used to feel kind of mazed, thinking of Bruce and the way he died.

One March evening about three months after the death of Bruce, I was driving down the M3 when suddenly I heard a noise in the back of the car. It was a frightening noise, and I couldn't place it at first. Then I realised it was the growling of a dog: a big dog, too, it sounded like. It was growling on a rising note – real aggressive. I was scared.

I stopped on the hard shoulder and looked in the back and then in the boot. Not a sausage. It was eerie: I knew I hadn't been mistaken. After a bit I got back in and drove on. The noise didn't come back and I didn't mention it to Mrs Forster.

But three days later, when I was driving home from Northampton on the A43 – a nasty bit of road near Juniper Hill – it suddenly began again. It was enough to scare the pants off anybody. In the back of my car was a large, savage dog, working itself up to attack – and nothing to be seen at all. You could even hear its claws on the seat and its coat brushing against the side. I stopped and jumped out; but then, after a few minutes, I got back in and drove on. The growling had stopped.

But it kept on coming back – and just when you were least expecting it. I'd find myself overtaking a lorry, or doing a hill start when suddenly this appalling growling broke out in the back. Grrrr-owf! Grrrr-owf! I nearly crashed twice. I was horribly frightened. It was beginning to keep me awake nights.

I wanted to talk to someone about it, but I mean how could you? My friends would say I was barmy with the death of Bruce. Mrs Forster wouldn't be any good. If my employers got to know they'd think I'd got a hallucinatory nervous breakdown – perhaps I had – and very likely sack me. 'You need a rest, Jevons.'

It went on, about twice a week or more, but I never got used to it. It fairly made my bowels loose when it came: it was right at the back of your head, you see, and you expected the brute to take you by the neck any minute.

In the end I decided I'd try changing the car. I spun them some sort of a fanny at the office about the clutch-plate not being too good, and they gave me another car while they took it off the road for attention. When they brought it back I said the new car was so much better; could I keep it? Well, the old one had done seventy thousand odd anyway, so they said all right. I really felt relieved – for about three days. Then, one night north of Newbury, the growling came again; and it was worse than ever. I couldn't stay in the car with it. It was like a wild animal. I stopped and got out and gave it half an hour. But it was getting me down. I was seriously beginning to wonder what would become of me.

About a week later, I was coming home unusually late. It had been a hard, frustrating day – a bad day, really. I turned into the wooded minor road near Hartley Wintney where Bruce had been killed. And it was coming down that road, in the woods, when the steering began to go funny. I slowed down. Bump, bump. It was pouring with rain. I got out my torch. The off-side rear tyre was flat.

Oh damn and shit! I thought. To have to change the wheel at this time of night, in all the rain! My shoes and hands will be filthy and I'll get wet through and probably get a cold or worse. Well, there was no help for it, so I opened the boot, lugged out the jack, the wheelbrace and the spare tyre, prised off the hub-cap and started in.

I'd done two of the nuts when I heard another car coming. The lights came round the bend, showing up the rods of rain, and then the car passed me and stopped. It was a grey Peugeot 309, and my torch showed the same discoloured patch on the boot. It was the car that had killed Bruce; I felt certain.

The driving door opened and a man got out into the road. I shone the torch on him and he flapped his hand, dazzled. I didn't like the look of him at all. He was big, heavy, about thirty, with a lot of black hair and a sort of nasty, oily smile. He came up to me.

'Oh! Got a puncture, 'ave yer?'

'Yes,' I said.

'Bit of a sod, that. Want any 'elp?'

'That's very kind of you.'

'What'll yer give me?'

This surprised me, of course, but after a moment I said, 'Well, how much do you want?'

'Well,' he answered, still with that horrible grin, 'I think I'll take what yer got.'

And with this he stepped forward and seized me, pushing his fingers down between my neck and the front of my shirt. His other fist was clenched.

Just at that moment the driver's-door of my car flew open – I honestly can't tell whether I'd shut it or not – and then the man staggered back, clutching at his throat and shouting, 'Keep it off! Keep it off!' It was like a dream – all unreal, I mean. He was ducking and weaving all over the place and trying to cover his head. As I looked at him, great rents appeared in his clothes. The growling and snarling was like I'd never heard. The man tried to kick out, and then grabbed at his ankle, screaming. I was crouching beside the car, wet through and terrified. Just as the man managed to lurch as far as his own car, a police car appeared and drew up.

One of the policemen went straight to the man and tried to speak to him. Then he supported him into the back of the police car. There was some talk I couldn't hear and then this policeman came over to me.

'Stand up, sir, please. Is this your car, sir?'

'Yes.'

'Where is your dog, sir, please?'

'I haven't got a dog.'

'Well, where is *the* dog?'

'I haven't seen a dog.'

'Well, sir, this man's been very badly bitten and mauled. It's a hospital job, this is. Are you saying it wasn't your dog that did it?'

'There isn't a dog. You can look in the car – anywhere.'

'The dog ran away?'

'I tell you – I haven't seen a dog.'

'Then are you saying, sir, that that dog came out of thin air?'

'Well, in effect, yes.'

'Oh, so there *was* a dog?'

'I tell you I didn't see a dog at all.'

An ambulance, its lights flashing, arrived and took the wretched mugger away. The policeman, having heard my story, seemed to decide that they were no nearer the truth, but that I was shocked and talking rubbish about there having been no dog. I left my car and they gave me a lift home. I was totally exhausted. Mrs F. gave me a cup of tea and I slept like a log.

Next day was Saturday. Over breakfast, planning to get a taxi to take me out to my car in the woods, I heard a ring at the bell. It was another policeman – a sergeant. I sat him down and he questioned me again. He said that I could be prosecuted for letting this savage dog attack the man. The man was in hospital. When I asked him point-blank, he told me the man was known to them and that he had a police record.

'But the dog must be destroyed, sir. Now I know you

were a bit shaken up last night, but this matter can't be overlooked.'

'I swear to you, sergeant, I have no dog and haven't had one for months. Let me call my landlady.'

Mrs Forster came in and she confirmed that I'd had no dog since Bruce had been killed.

'Well, sir,' said the sergeant at last, and, so it seemed to me, reluctantly. 'I'd rather it *had* been your dog. Then we'd all know where we were.'

'Where we were?' I said. 'I'd like to know that, too.'

He left, shaking his head. I set off to get my car. All the tools were still in the road and it was untouched.

Since then, the noises in the car have stopped altogether. I've got another dog, another collie called Cracker. He's great. I feel a new man.

I've only told this to one other person; my drinking friend Jack Vincent, who teaches Eng. Lit. at the Poly. We'd had three pints each when I told him in the bar at The George one night. I felt I had to tell someone or bust. I thought he'd laugh at me or tell me I was trying to fool him. But he didn't. He heard me out in silence and he stayed silent when I'd finished.

'D'you believe me?' I asked him.

'Yes, I think I do,' he answered. Then he said, 'It is nought good a sleeping hound to wake.'

'What?'

'Chaucer, old boy. "Troilus and Criseyde".'

TAIL

Bill James

There was an agreement. Brian and Jill had spelled it out together one night, more than a year ago. They told each other it was for the sake of the children. And Brian told himself that, too. But he knew it was for his own sake. He must not lose Jill. To keep her he had accepted terms. They would be friends, living together with their family. For passion she would go elsewhere. It was terribly regrettable, she said, but something had died. It could happen in a marriage. Look at some of their friends! She still loved him dearly, but was not 'in love' with him any longer. She had met someone else, a little older than Brian, as it happened, and also married, but none of that seemed to matter. They had fallen 'in love'.

Obviously, Brian had been hurt, but did not really accept the difference between love and 'in love'. Or, at least, did not believe that side of it would last. He would wait it out. And so, the agreement. He considered it a workable, not necessarily humiliating pact and, even at the end, remained convinced that nobody reasonable would have forseen such loss and violence.

When the arrangement began, Jill used to offer some more or less plausible tale to cover the times she was absent: shopping, a drink with Amy. Then she stopped that. It obviously sickened her to lie. She had a wonderful honesty. It was one of the things he loved her for. These days she would say only that she would be out in the evening or, more usually, the middle of the day and afternoon, and he asked no questions because none was necessary, and because this silence had become part of the agreement.

Other extra, unspoken clauses to the treaty had also established themselves. For instance, he noticed that she never dressed up in her smartest outfits to go to these meetings, nor wore any of the best jewellery he had bought her. Brian saw she did not want to rub his nose in it by making herself festooned and special for someone else, and he felt grateful. He could not tell her that, though.

In fact, it was when Brian and Jill called the babysitter and they went out as a couple to a restaurant or party at a friend's place that she wore her best outfits, and appeared at her most gloriously elegant. A room full of people shone when she was among them, shone *because* she was among them. He had always adored her for this quality, and did now. Brian was proud to be married to her. Just as much as feelings and sex, her allure and brilliance were the essence of Jill, and these she did not withdraw from him. This was why he could abide by the agreement. She remained his. The wondrous public side of her belonged to him, still. Ask anyone what they thought of first when Jill's name was mentioned and they would say her vivid radiance in company. He could read envy of him in men's faces. Lately, she would give extra care to her appearance when, with Brian and the children, she visited his parents. He knew his mother and father understood now what an asset to him Jill was. Both Brian's daughters looked like her, fortunately, and, even at ten and thirteen, it was obvious that they, too, would be beautiful women.

Naturally, it was part of the agreement, one of the formally spelled-out parts, that if he found somebody else, he would be free to seek fulfilment with her, though observing a like care for preservation of the household. But Brian was sure he would never want that. Unthinkable. He saw that his certainty on this used to enrage Jill now and then. It possibly increased her proper and commendable sense of guilt. But he could not change. Jill was the only woman he wanted, and, if necessary, she would be his on the present hard but bearable conditions. Once, and never afterwards, she tried to explain what it was that had drawn her from him to this other man. What she said seemed rather imprecise to Brian. Perhaps she avoided too much clarity for fear of injuring him more. She would be like that. What it appeared to add up to was that the lover radiated unceasingly a ferocious desire for her. This was the word she picked, *ferocious*. She spoke it without hesitation, and had obviously selected it very carefully a while before and kept it ready for this declaration. Brian was embarrassed by it rather than injured. She sounded absurd, he felt. Yet she said this man's passion had left her no choice. Brian did not protest, though he longed to say he, too, had desire for her. Didn't his humane tolerance of the agreement prove this?

When the arrangement was new, he did not allow himself to think very much about where the two the them went on their sorties, and at that stage he would never have tailed her, or had her professionally tailed. Although this was certainly not expressly banned by their agreement, it would have been shady then. In those days, Brian totally despised snooping. He assumed they generally went to an early lunch in a restaurant, and then somewhere else. Unseemly to speculate on that, and probably unhealthy. She liked to be home soon after the children returned from school.

What he took care never to do on days when she had obviously been to a rendezvous was suggest they eat out together somewhere that evening. This would have been cruelty, forcing her to consume two big restaurant meals in a day, and seeming to score over the lunch date by getting her to dress up for dinner. It was certainly not for him to, as it were, punish her. He had told her once or twice that he was 'not in the business of blame'.

Yet sometimes after she had been capering somewhere with her lover in the day, Jill would seem to detect Brian's delicacy and grow defiant and combative in her wise shame. She herself would insist they summon the babysitter right away and go to the very best restaurant they knew. It was as if she were insulted by his considerateness and wanted to destroy it. Perhaps she thought he believed his gentlemanliness made him superior. This was plainly unjust.

Then, in the restaurant, looking brilliant, she would talk and radiate at full power, and anyone watching would surely have supposed them alight with joy in each other, perhaps even lovers, not man and wife. This would thrill him. This was Jill as Brian's, her jewellery very much in place. Always on these occasions she would order expensively, and took something from every course. She would eat little – probably *could* eat little – but this did not matter. As Brian saw it, wanted to see it, she was demonstrating that she was his and therefore had not the least need to stint. Her extravagance was possessiveness. As far as he could tell from studying her eyes and face, the vivacity was real, not merely acted out. He would not believe that, behind it all, she was venomously comparing this outing to the one she had been on earlier that day as preamble to sex.

Now and then, they would bump into friends in these places and perhaps make up a four or even push tables together for a party of six or eight. The more the better for Jill. She would grow livelier and livelier and, in Brian's opinion, anyway, lovelier, too. No, it was not only his opinion. He could see this view endorsed in the eyes of the other men, and even in the eyes of some of the other women. Jill had this wonderful ability to bring glamour to a group, without causing jealousy. This was the girl he had married and cherished, regardless. He knew he was lucky.

On one of these evenings, they came across a group of dining friends at Claud's Bistro, and, while they were rearranging tables, he felt a hand, probably the back of a hand, a woman's hand judging by the size, pressed for a second, possibly a fraction more, very firmly against the inside of his left, upper thigh, and high. His initial thought was that it had happened accidentally, in the minor confusions of already heavily aperitifed people moving furniture. Soon, though, he realised that this could not be; the duration of the contact was too long, its nature too deliberate, too questing and cogent. He decided, yearned to decide, that it had been Jill. Was she telling him in a sudden, uncontrollable, almost shy way that she belonged to him after all; altogether belonged to him, and not just her public self, however worthwhile that public self might be? Perhaps her affair and therefore the absurd agreement were over. Always he had known time would put matters right.

But soon he came to recognise that, although Jill had been close as they all wrestled with tables and chairs, she was not close enough to touch him. It was Amy, Jeremy Postern's strapping young wife, who had been nearest on his left. By now, the hand was withdrawn and they all prepared to sit down. There had been no apology or joke from her about the contact, which seemed to confirm – to confirm needlessly – that it had not been unintentional. But Amy seemed to make no attempt to be seated next to him during the meal, and, when he talked to her and looked at her as the evening went on, he could find no personal message, no easily readable equivalent in her blue-black eyes of knuckles calculatedly nudging his nuts. By then, anyway, Jill had begun to sparkle in her unique way, beguiling everyone, and particularly Brian. It still saddened him that this little slice of pressure had not come from her, but an agreement was an agreement, and he could take his customary solid pleasure in her social being. It was not ferocious pleasure, yet valid, surely.

A couple of days later, he began to feel that only foolish, smug optimism had made him imagine Jill wished to return. In fact, he had been guilty of trivialising the agreement they had so conscientiously worked out together. Now, he re-ran in his head the details of the agreement, and decided he did not give it due seriousness. Jill might be correct to resent his patronising attitude, particularly, for instance, Brian's pious, dismissive treatment of the major clause offering him equivalent sexual liberty.

Early one evening, when he was having an after-work drink with Jeremy Postern and other business friends in The Old Barn cocktail bar, he left them briefly, went to one of the hotel's public booths and telephoned Amy. She seemed warm, pleased to hear him, unsurprised. He wondered if they might meet one evening, and she thought they might. They arranged a time. Brian went back to the group in the bar feeling not excited or victorious but, yes, more *wholesome* – that was the state – more wholesome than for a long while.

Amy and he seemed to need no preliminaries. It was as if they had been waiting for each other. She went halves with him on a bottle of Dubonnet and the charge for a room overnight in a small, cheap hotel, though they would be using it only for a few hours in the early evening. After they had made fierce love – yes, he had to concede, even *ferocious* love – and were lying relaxed on the bed, he felt he should reassure Amy about the care he would always take with her reputation. He explained that he had telephoned her only when certain Jeremy could not be at home.

'Oh, the bleak sod wouldn't care,' Amy replied. She sounded appallingly defeated and miserable. 'We go our own ways.'

'You don't like that?'

Hurriedly, she turned towards him: 'Darling, of course I do. I couldn't be here with you now, otherwise, could I?'

'You're just being polite?'

She did not answer. In a while, though, she said: 'Isn't it the same with you and Jill?'

'Good God, no. I could not tolerate the idea of her seeing, screwing somebody else.'

'Ah, I love jealousy in a man,' she cried, moving her hand on to his thigh again, though this time the front of her hand and higher still, then higher. 'It means he cares. It's because you can throb with jealousy, Brian, that you're so damn irresistible and sexy. You're not the kind who would doze through a marriage. God, but Jill's so lucky.'

This opening meeting with Amy changed him, gave him vision. Jesus, did Jill think he did not care, because he showed no rage and accepted the agreement? Was this why she would never return fully to him? But he did care. He must show it. He was not like Jeremy – and like so many husbands Brian knew: husbands who by sexual indifference forced a loveless wife to seek fulfilment elsewhere. The next time Jill said she would be out for the afternoon, he decided he would follow her. He still loathed the idea of spying, but now he had come to loathe even more the idea of being passive: of 'dozing through their marriage' and, so, pushing her towards another man. He would blow this disgusting, bloodless agreement to smithereens. But agreements were just words and sentiments. He wanted something solid to smash, and he needed a good look at the opposition. It had been an understood part of the agreement that he asked nothing about the man Jill saw. Now, though, Brian had to identify him.

To tail her would involve taking time off from the business, and he could certainly not afford to do that very often. Although the firm was successful, it was very much a one-man operation, and he would not neglect it simply to dog his wife and her boyfriend week after week. But possibly things would not take that long.

On both occasions that he watched them they began by going to a grubby little restaurant for lunch. He could have predicted it. This would be another reason for her not dressing up. Wearing one of her authentic ensembles, she would have looked outlandish in this place. Generous to call it a restaurant. This was a café in a drab street, with 'Heavy Breakfast – £1.50' scrawled in thin, white lettering on the window. He saw people who looked like clerks or shop assistants going in at lunchtime, and some men in dungarees. Never would Brian have taken a woman there, and certainly not a woman like Jill, even in run-of-the-mill clothes.

At first, he thought lover-boy must be short of money. In a while, though, Brian saw the cleverness. The pair were unlikely to meet anyone they knew in such poor surroundings, and especially not Jill. Secrecy was more important than cuisine.

Following her was tricky, of course. Jill would soon notice his car behind her, so he hired different vehicles each time: once an Escort, next a Cavalier. Their drill seemed to be to meet in a waste ground, municipal car park, then walk to the café. First, though, he went to her VW for a few minutes and they kissed and talked, all excited smiles, one arm around the other's shoulders, as if they had fought their way back together across ice floes, mountains and volcanoes after God knew how many years of forced separation. Probably, they were here every week.

Each time he tailed her, Brian waited in the hired car not far from their house until she left at about 1 pm. On the first outing, it was really difficult, because he did not know where she was going, and he had to keep close enough to stick, yet avoid being recognised in her mirror. When she entered the car park, he quickly selected a spot for himself far from the one she made for. He had to take his eyes off her then, as he parked. When he looked again it was just in time to see the back view of a middle-height man as he left from a Toyota close to her car, walked the few steps, opened her passenger door and climbed in. To Brian, this appeared a routine: it was that kind of confident stepping out and decisive opening of the door. This bastard could count on a welcome. He had had a lot of welcomes already.

Brian was a distance from them, had to be, but he saw the heads go together for a prolonged thank-God-we-made-it kiss, and then could observe happy grins and laughter, hers. The back of the man's head was still towards Brian, mostly grey, but cut short and bristly in a young thruster style. This was how Brian had to think of him on that first occasion – as the man, or lover-boy. Boy? Christ, he had to be at least ten years older than Brian. This was plain at first glimpse, and it hurt. She could prefer someone that age? Only subsequently did Brian discover his name was Lowther, and, quite fortunately, where he lived.

On the second expedition, it was easier. When she set out from home, he did not know as a certainty she would make for the same place, but it soon became apparent that this was her route again. As they approached the car park, he saw the Toyota waiting, this time with a space available right alongside. She made for that. Once more Brian found a place far off. As the man moved to her car today, Brian was able to get a good, thirty-second view of him face-on; a round cheerful-looking face, with heavy eyebrows. The shifty glow of Indian summer was about him. He could easily have had the eyebrows trimmed, but must feel they were a key part of his image, giving him definition and weight. His face was full now of . . . full now of what Brian would have liked to dismiss as raw, lucky-old-me triumph. After all, this was someone in his fifties at least, all set for a long afternoon with an attractive woman of thirty-four. And he would manage it on the greasy cheap. Yet, horrified, Brian found he could not honestly describe what he saw like that. He saw . . . well, Christ, yes, he saw love there – maybe ferocious, maybe just intense, but in any case enough to frighten him. He sensed the power of their relationship, could almost admire it, and could certainly envy it.

He directed himself back to hostility and hate. This man's clothes were like some 1970s sports commentator's – three-quarter-length sheepskin coat and a crimson scarf. For his age he was nimble, Brian could not deny that. Of course he was bloody nimble. The relic skipped with pleasure at getting in amongst someone else's wife. Even now, during this greetings kiss, there was no knowing where their spare hands were.

But, God, Amy had it right and Brian could switch on the jealousy. He might tell her about this whole damn sequence, as testament to his vehemence. For the moment, today, Brian sat still: perhaps there was still a tremor or two of power left in the agreement. He wondered if Jill had told this old lad about it. That would make him even more hearty and nimble. The creep knew he had a nice clear track.

When they were ready to go and eat they would have another sweet, close, chuckly time, obviously sorting out their coins for the ticket machine – so chummy. The man walked over to pay. No, perhaps not as much as fifty, and presentable, unquestionably, despite the eyebrows. But, of course presentable. Wasn't it a rotten insult to Jill to think otherwise? Brian saw it would be absurd to feel jealousy if the rival was a washout. He looked as if he might be assistant manager of a Social Security office, or a newsagent. How could he get this time off continually?

They fixed their tickets to the car windows then strolled to the café. On both days that he watched, she took his arm for a while, as though feeling anonymous in this downmarket end of the town. But then she would suddenly let go and put a little gap between them, probably thinking that, downmarket or not, acquaintances could be driving through and might spot her. To be spotted at all would be bad, but walking arm in arm was a total give-away. They would hold the distance for a few paces and then drift close again. These lechers could not bear not to be touching. He might put his palm on her back or behind, really finger-digging the cleft through her clothes, despite daylight, and she might hold his arm again for a few strides. Eventually, they went out of sight of the car park.

On his first trip, Brian bought himself a ticket and, when it seemed safe, walked after them. By now they were quite a way ahead, and they never looked back, anyway. He did not know where they were going, of course, but was just in time to see them turn into the café's doorway. He was glad he witnessed it, because he would never have believed any man would use a place like this for a tryst, and Brian might have walked past, in view from inside through the window. In fact, he crossed the street and loitered until a group of people would shield him as he passed. He had time for a few swift glances only. They were at a table far from the window and were too interested in each other to watch what was happening outside. Brian continued on, had a quick sandwich and tea in another café, and then found a different way back to the waste ground via side streets. Their cars were still there, unoccupied.

On the second occasion, Brian knew where they were going when they quit the cars and did not follow. It was too risky. He had brought a thermos flask of tea and a full picnic meal this time, with plastic cutlery and plates: two turkey drumsticks, tomatoes, bread rolls, cheese and yoghurt. How those two managed to spin out a meal for so long in a place like that, he did not understand, but he knew they would. He also knew now what the procedure would be later. They would return smiling and chatting and arm in arm, as though having forgotten about the danger of being seen. Perhaps the food had made them blasé, even that kind of food. Possibly customers were allowed to send out for wine, since such a dump could have no licence. At any rate, they looked euphoric. They would climb into the front of his Toyota and he would drive to a more secluded part of the car park. It was late afternoon by now and there were a lot of spaces. Brian made sure his car was parked near the edge of the waste ground adjacent to the main road, certain they would not relocate to this very visible area.

The first time he tailed it was late November, and the second, early December, so that, by about half past three darkness had begun to come down. By four it was almost night, and also by four the Toyota was steamed up. No doubt there had been movement from the front to the back seats, though Brian could not see that from so far off. No need to see. Brian knew it. Afterwards, her lover would drive the Toyota back to alongside the VW and they would leave. Lots of waves, like emigration.

While they were still at lunch on the second outing, and after he had finished his own, Brian strolled to the Toyota, took its registration number and glanced inside. He had a business acquaintance who, for a mighty fee, could somehow trace the owners of cars via number plates. Fortunately, however, this would be unnecessary because Brian saw an opened envelope on top of the dashboard, and it was now he learned lover-boy's name was G. Lowther, and where he lived. He made another note. Brian thought this one looked like a Gordon rather than a Geoffrey or a Grant.

After both these long spells of duty, Brian went back to the office to make up for time lost. Some routines really had to continue. But, obviously, his mind was badly troubled and he did not operate well. To clear the backlog papers and deal with calls on the Answerphone, he had to stay late for several nights after the second excursion with them; and, of course, there was now another rather central matter to be dealt with, quite unconnected with the office.

Returning home very late after one of these business sessions, Brian was surprised to find Jill still up. She had seemed desolated recently and would go to bed early.

'Jeremy Postern rang,' she said.

'Does he want me to call him back? At this hour?'

'He rang *me*,' she said.
'Oh, yes?'
'Amy told him you and she have an affair going.'
'But why would she do that?' Brian replied.
'To make him jealous, I expect. Force him to want her.'
'But he couldn't care less,' Brian replied.
'He's frantic. He asked me what we can do about it, he and I.'
'Just like Jeremy.'
'I won't tolerate it. I'm leaving you, Brian. Tonight. Now. For keeps. I've sent the girls by taxi to my mother's.'
'But, Jill, darling, why?' he cried. 'It was only the agreement.'
'The agreement is finished.'
'It is?'
She wept. 'I've no need of it any longer. The man I was seeing is dead.'
'Oh, dear. Poor Jill.'
'Murdered outside his house. Brutally knifed.'
'I think I read about this in the papers.'
'What does that mean?'
'I don't follow you,' he replied. Then he changed this: 'I don't understand you.'
'How did you know that the man you read about was George?'
He chuckled mildly for a second. 'No, no, Jill, I meant I had read about a man being knifed near his house. Appalling. George?'
'So, I'm going, for good,' she replied. She went out to her car. He walked urgently after her, and saw that the VW was loaded with cases. The car looked lonely without the Toyota alongside. Jill turned: 'Oh, Brian, how in God's name could you betray me with someone like Amy Postern?'
'She taught me the way to hold on to you, my love,' he replied as she drove off. She did not wave.

A SAFE PLACE

Anna Reynolds

Once upon a time there was a girl, and she lived in a small house with stripped pine floors, stripped pine furniture, and lots of dead flowers that she paid a fortune for. She didn't mind the expense, because they hid a multitude of sins. She worked in an office as a secretary and she was given no responsibility except franking the mail and taking dictation from the Managing Director, who was up to some shady business, she was sure. The air in his office was filled with curls of blue smoke from his Benson and Hedges cigarettes and he had a bar made out of mahogany, with many crystal decanters set on its surface. He was a small, fat man, with photographs on his desk of his fat wife and fat children. He also had a girly calendar with women playing peek-a-boo with feathers and negligées, smiling flatly down at passengers through the office.

The girl was often bored with her work but she didn't really mind that because it gave her plenty of time to daydream of a better life and she read romantic sagas throbbing with powerful, glamorous women and strong, square-jawed men. The covers of these books even had helpful pictures of these women and men in case the descriptions inside didn't give you enough clues.

She had a boyfriend, this girl, and he worked in a fitness centre. He liked to work out a lot himself, and he often sat opposite the mirror in restaurants because he liked to gently flex his pecs and biceps underneath his crisp, white shirt and watch the candlelight illuminate his clean cheekbones and his narrow, grey eyes. His hair was cut sharply and his shoes were always well shined and polished. He insisted that they live in separate flats and he liked her to look fit.

Everyone at the office liked this girl. She never lost her temper, never appeared in a ferociously bad mood, always made coffee when asked and didn't wince at the MD's leers and innuendos. She was a patient, sweet-natured girl and she lived a stripped-pine sort of life.

The girls in the office often spoke about her quietly, wonderingly. However does she manage to be so well-turned out, so unflustered, so even-tempered, they asked each other? How does she cope with a child and a boy-friend and a job?

They had heard all about her little daughter, Jennie. Jennie was six years old, and went to a good school in Wimbledon near the girl's house. She had straight, shiny perfect blonde hair, like her mother, and round blue eyes, like her mother. They hadn't seen a photograph because she kept forgetting to bring one in. They forgave her this because she obviously had a lot to think about. She had an excellent nanny, who was a friend of hers, and she spent the weekends and evenings with her daughter and her boyfriend, who adored the daughter too. They must make a lovely couple, the other girls said enviously. So attractive, so shiny, so perfect.

They had not met the boyfriend because he worked different hours and so could not spare the time to come and pick her up from work but they had heard all about him, oh yes. His job at the fitness centre, his paternal values, his enthusiasm to do the washing-up and the ironing and how he had been the first to leap out of bed and change nappies when Jennie was a baby. Was it a difficult birth, they had asked her, thinking into the future? She had blushed and said no, and they had noticed that she was reluctant to talk about . . . well, personal things.

They thought of her as a girl but she was really thirty-two years of age. But her hair was so girlishly, charmingly tied in a pony tail, so gleamingly, brushingly pulled back, revealing her shiny, youthful skin, her small, neat, perfect ears, her round blue eyes, her neat, small, rosy mouth, that they always thought of her as a girl. Her boyfriend didn't believe in marriage, she said, apologetically, carefully, in their lunchtime chats over a tub of cottage cheese turned pink with salmon flakes. He felt that their relationship was stable and perfect already and why change it? Why indeed? The girls nodded. Why change such a perfect thing, why risk it, why alter the smooth balance for, after all, no good reason?

She kept herself to herself in the office and the girls understood this. After all, she had a lot to cope with. Sometimes she took days off to go to her daughter's school play, or the parents' evenings. Or to take Jennie to the dentist. They thought of her as a role model; they could imagine themselves in her in five years' time; so neat, so shiny, so organised.

One day the girl got up and, according to her usual routine, put on the coffee percolator, stood in the shower, dressed immaculately – no snagged tights here – and sat in front of her Ikea pine dressing-table putting on her Beauty Without Cruelty make-up. The natural look, just enough, but not too much. No. That would never do.

And then the phone rang. Now, at eight o'clock in the morning, this was very unusual.

'May I speak with Miss or Mrs Hardy?' said a timorous voice.

'Speaking,' said the girl. 'Who's calling, please?'

She'd sometimes forget that she wasn't at work because the phone hardly ever rang at home. She had a few very close friends and they were mostly girls at work.

'This is your daughter speaking,' said the strange little voice. 'Remember me?'

On the tube the girl went past her stop and had to catch the tube back again. She went up the 'Down' stairs and rushed out of the station unusually flushed.

At work she managed to mangle up the photocopier, set the franking machine for the wrong date and spill coffee over the MD within the first half-hour. Everyone was very surprised and unnerved, because the girl was never late, never hurried, never out of place. Her hair was loose and uncombed and her eyeliner seemed to be crooked.

A lunchtime she flew out of the office, knocking over a

pot-plant in her wake. This was also unsettling because she tended to all the office plants and indeed cooed over and cosseted them rather lovingly.

She sat in the café waiting for her daughter to come to meet her. The girl who eventually turned up was not at all expected. She didn't have neat shiny hair or smooth, ironed, neutral clothes. She stormed in rather noisily, wearing a bright purple fringed dress which covered her bottom – but only just – and thick black tights and enormous shoes like big boats. She wore aggressive make-up and her hair was fixed on her head like a cockatoo. Her first words were, 'Why did you abandon me?' She sat down fiercely and waited for the answer.

'Oh, Jennie . . .' said the girl, her head in her hands.

'I'm not called Jennie. I'm called Andrea,' said the new daughter.

'Oh, Andrea,' said the girl. 'I was sixteen. I was – your age. I wasn't allowed to keep you, you see.'

The new daughter sat thinking for a minute or two. Then – 'I would have fought like hell, to keep a child. I'm dying for a child. I wouldn't do that to anybody, leave them in the care of the world.'

Then – 'Have you got other kids? Ones that you did keep?'

The girl swallowed and said, 'No.'

'Have you got a husband? Or a boyfriend?'

No.

'What do you live like? Have you got a house, or a flat? Do you go to work? What do you do?'

Stop, please stop! I don't have a life. I have a nice pine house, a little house at the end of the world and I don't have a life.

Would you like to see my house?

Back on the tube to Wimbledon, the last outpost of humanity. The door opened smoothly. The pine floors, stripped over and over again free of any life. The smooth, white, painted walls, sterilised of any colour. No house room for mistakes here.

The brand new daughter walked all around the little house. 'Isn't it neat?' she cried. 'Is it not tidy, shiny, tasteful?'

The girl had no answer for she was watching her huge, boisterous new daughter, who had the shoulders of a bruiser and the wild energy of discovery.

'I can see why you gave me away,' said the daughter at last. 'There simply isn't room for me here. I am not tidy, nor shiny, nor should I ever wish to be.' And with that she left the small house noisily, clumpingly.

The girl sat there for a long time and then she stood up. She straightened a print that the daughter had knocked awry in her wake and she smoothed down the covers on the sofa. She swallowed.

THE CASE OF THE PARR CHILDREN

Antonia Fraser

'I've come about the children.'

The woman who stood outside the door of the flat, her finger poised to ring the bell again, looked desperate. She also looked quite unknown to the owner of the flat, Jemima Shore. It was ten o'clock on Sunday morning; an odd time for anyone to be paying a social call on the celebrated television reporter. Jemima Shore had no children. Outside her work she led a very free and very private existence. As she stood at the door, unusually dishevelled, pulling a dark blue towelling robe round her, she had time to wonder rather dazedly: Whose children? Why here? Before she decided that the stranger had rung the wrong bell of the wrong flat, and very likely the wrong house in Holland Park.

'I've come about the children.'

The woman before her was panting slightly as she repeated the words. But then Jemima Shore's flat was on the top floor. It was her appearance which on closer inspection was odd: she looked smudged and dirty like a charcoal drawing which had been abandoned. Her beltless mackintosh had presumably once been white; as had perhaps her ancient tennis shoes with their gaping canvas, and her thick woollen socks. The thin dark dress she wore beneath her mackintosh, hem hanging down, gave the impression of being too old for her until Jemima realised that it was the dress itself which was decrepit. Only her hair showed any sign of care: that had at least been brushed. Short and brown, it hung down straight on either side of her face: in this case the style was too young.

The woman before Jemima might have been a tramp. Then there was the clink of a bottle at her feet as she moved uneasily towards Jemima. In a brown paper bag at her feet were the remains of a picnic which had clearly been predominantly alcoholic. The image of the tramp was confirmed.

'Jemima Shore, Investigator?' she gasped. 'You've *got* to help me.' And she repeated for the third time: 'You see, I've come about the children.'

Jemima recoiled slightly. It was true that she was billed by this title in her programmes of serious social reportage. It was also true that the general public had from time to time mistaken her for a real investigator as a result. Furthermore, lured by the magic spell of know-all television, people had on occasion brought her problems to solve; and she had on occasion solved them. Nevertheless, early Sunday morning, well before the first cup of coffee, seemed an inauspicious moment for such an appeal. In any case, by the sound of it, the woman needed a professional social worker rather than an amateur investigator.

Jemima decided that the lack of coffee could at least be remedied. Pulling her robe still further around her, and feeling more than slightly cross, she led the way into her elegant little kitchen. The effect of the delicate pink formica surfaces was to make the tramp-woman look grubbier than ever. At which point her visitor leant forward on her kitchen stool, covered in pretty rose-coloured denim, and started to sob loudly and uncontrollably into her hands. Tears trickled between her fingers. Jemima noticed with distaste that the fingernails too were dirty. Coffee was by now not so much desirable as essential. Jemima proceeded first to make it, and then to administer it.

Ten minutes later she found herself listening to a very strange story indeed. The woman who was telling it described herself as Mrs Catharine Parr.

'Yes, just like the wretched Queen who lost her head, and I'm just as wretched, I'm quite lost too.' Jemima raised her eyebrows briefly at the historical inaccuracy – hadn't Catharine Parr, sixth wife of Henry VIII, died in her bed? But as Mrs Parr rushed on with her dramatic tale, she reflected that here was a woman who probably embellished everything with unnecessary flourishes. Mrs Parr was certainly wretched enough; that went without question. Scotland. She had come overnight from Scotland. Hence of course both the mackintosh and the thin dress, even the picnic (although the empty wine bottles remained unexplained). Hence the early hour, for Mrs Parr had come straight from Euston Station, off her sleeper. And now it was back to the children again.

At this point, Jemima Shore managed at last to get a word in edgeways: 'Whose children? Your children?'

Mrs Parr, tears checked, looked at Jemima as though she must already know the answer to that question: 'Why, the *Parr* children of course. Don't you remember the case of the Parr children? There was a lot about it on television,' she added reproachfully.

'The Parr children: yes, I think I do remember something – your children, I suppose.'

To Jemima's surprise there was a pause. Then Mrs Parr said with great solemnity:

'Miss Shore, that's just what I want you to find out. I just don't *know* whether they're my children or not. I just don't *know*.'

'I think,' said Jemima Shore, Investigator, resignedly drinking her third cup of coffee, 'You had better tell me all about it from the beginning.'

Oddly enough Jemima did genuinely remember something about the episode. Not from television, but from the newspapers where it had been much discussed, notably in the *Guardian*; and Jemima was a *Guardian* reader. It had been a peculiarly rancorous divorce case. The elderly judge had come down heavily on the side of the father. Not only had he taken the unusual step of awarding Mr Parr care and custody of the two children of the marriage – mere babies – but he had also summed up the case in full for the benefit of the Press.

In particular he had dwelt venomously on the imperfections of Mrs Parr and her 'trendy amoral Bohemianism unsuitable for contact with any young creature'. This was because Mrs Parr had admitted having an affair with a gypsy or something equally exotic. She now proposed to take her children off with him for the glorious life of the open road; which, she suggested, would enable her children to grow up uninhibited loving human beings. Mr Parr responded with a solid bourgeois proposition, including a highly responsible Nannie, a general atmosphere of nursery tea now, private schools later. Columnists had had a field day for a week or two, discussing the relative merits of bourgeois and Bohemian life-styles for children. On the whole Jemima herself had sympathised with the warm-blooded Mrs Parr.

It transpired that Jemima's recollection of the case was substantially correct. Except that she had forgotten the crucial role played by the so-called Nannie; in fact no Nannie but a kind of poor relation, a trained nurse named Zillah. It was Zillah who had spoken with calm assurance of the father's love for his children, reluctantly of the selfish flightiness of the mother. She had known her cousin Catharine all her life, she said, although their material circumstances had been very different. She pronounced with regret that in her opinion Catharine Parr was simply not fitted to have sole responsibility for young children. It was one of the reasons which had prompted her to leave her nursing career in order to look after the Parr babies.

Since Zillah was clearly a detached witness who had the welfare of the children at heart, her evidence was regarded as crucial by the judge. He contrasted Catharine and Zillah: 'two young women so outwardly alike, so inwardly different'. He made this also a feature of his summing-up. 'Miss Zillah Roberts, who has had none of the benefits of money and education of the mother in the case, has nevertheless demonstrated the kind of firm moral character most appropriate to the care of infants . . . etc. etc.'

In vain Mrs Parr had exploded in court:

'Don't believe her. She's his mistress! They're sleeping together. She's been jealous of me all her life. She always wanted everything I had, my husband, now my children.'

Such wild unsubstantiated talk did Mrs Parr no good at all, especially in view of her own admitted 'uninhibited and loving' behaviour. If anything the judge's summing-up gained in vinegar from the interruption.

Mrs Parr skated over the next part of her story. Deprived of her children, she had set off for the south of Ireland with her lover. Jemima had the impression, listening to her, that drink had played a considerable part in the story – drink and perhaps despair too. Nor did Mrs Parr enlarge on the death of her lover, except to say that he had died as he had lived: 'violently'. As a result Jemima had no idea whether Mrs Parr regretted her bold leap out of the bourgeois nest. All she discovered was that Mrs Parr had had no contact whatsoever with her children for seven years. Neither sought nor proffered. Not sought because Mr Parr had confirmed Mrs Parr's suspicions by marrying Zillah the moment his divorce became absolute: 'and *she* would never have permitted it. Zillah.' Not proffered, of course, because Mrs Parr had left no address behind her.

'I had to make a new life. I wouldn't take any money from him. They'd taken my children away from me and I had to make a new life.'

It was only after the death of Mrs Parr's lover that, destitute and friendless, she had returned to England. Contacting perforce her ex-husband's lawyer for funds of some sort, she had discovered to her astonishment that Mr Parr had died suddenly several months earlier. The lawyers had been trying in their dignified and leisurely fashion to contact his first wife, the mother of his children. In the meantime the second Mrs Parr, Zillah, the children's ex-Nannie and step-mother had taken them off to a remote corner of the Scottish Highlands. As she put it to the lawyer, she intended 'to get them and me away from it all'. The lawyer had demurred with the question of the children's future outstanding. But Zillah, with that same quiet air of authority which had swayed the divorce court judge, convinced him. It might be months before the first Mrs Parr was contacted, she pointed out. In the meantime they had her address. And the children's.

'And suddenly there I was!' exclaimed Mrs Catharine

Parr to Jemima Shore, the vehemence returning to her voice. 'But it was too late.'

'Too late?'

'Too late for Zillah. You see, Miss Shore, Zillah was dead. She was drowned in a boating accident in Scotland. It was too late for Zillah.' Jemima, sensing the depth of Mrs Parr's bitterness, realised that what she really meant was: too late for vengeance.

Even then, Mrs Parr's troubles were not over. The encounter with the children had been even more upsetting. Two children, Tamsin nearly nine and Tara nearly eight, who confronted her with scared and hostile eyes. They were being cared for at the lodge which Zillah had so precipitately rented. A local woman from the village, responsible for the caretaking of the lodge, had volunteered. Various suggestions had been made to transfer the children to somewhere less lonely, attended by less tragic memories. However, Tamsin and Tara had shown such extreme distress at the idea of moving away from their belongings and the home they knew that the plan had been abandoned. In the meantime their real mother had also announced her arrival.

So Mrs Parr took the sleeper to Inverness.

'But when I got to Scotland I didn't recognise them!' cried Mrs Parr in a return to her dramatic style. 'So I want you to come back to Scotland with me and *interview* them. Find out who they are. You're an *expert* interviewer: I've seen you on television. That programme about refugee children. You talk to them. I beg you, Miss Shore. You see before you a desperate woman and a fearful mother.'

'But were you likely to recognise them?' enquired Jemima rather dryly. 'I mean, you hadn't seen either of them for seven years. How old was Tamsin then – eighteen months? Tara – what – six months?'

'It wasn't a question of *physical* recognition, I assure you. In a way, they *looked* more or less as I expected. Fair. Healthy. She'd looked after them alright, Zillah, whoever they are. She always looked after people, Zillah. That's how she got him, of course.'

'Then why —' began Jemima hastily.

Mrs Parr leant forward and said in a conspiratorial

tone: 'It was spiritual recognition I meant. Nothing spoke to me and said: These are my children. In fact a voice deep in me cried out: Zillah! These are Zillah's children. This is Zillah's revenge. Even from the grave, she won't let me have my own children.' She paused for effect.

'You see, Zillah had this sister Kitty. We were cousins, I think I told you. Quite close cousins even though we had been brought up so differently. That's how Zillah came to look after the children in the first place: she wanted a proper home, she said, after the impersonality of nursing. But that didn't satisfy Zillah. She was always on at me to do something about this sister and her family – as though their awful lives were my fault!'

She went on: 'Kitty had two little girls, almost exactly the same ages as my two. Quite fair then, though not as fair as Zillah and not as fair as my children. But there was a resemblance, everyone said so. People sometimes took them for my children. I suppose our relationship accounted for it. Kitty was a wretched creature but physically we were not unalike. Anyway, Zillah thought the world of these babies and was always having them round. Kitty was unhappily married: I believe the husband ran off before the last baby was born. Suddenly, looking at this pair, I thought: little cuckoos. Zillah has taken her own nieces, and put them into my nest —'

'— Which you had left of your own accord.' But Jemima did not say the words aloud. Instead she asked with much greater strength:

'But *why*?'

'The money! That's why,' exclaimed Mrs Parr in triumph. 'The Parr money in trust for them. Parr Biscuits. Doesn't that ring a bell? The money only went to the descendants of Ephraim Parr. *She* wouldn't have got a penny – except what *he* left her. Her nieces had no Parr blood either. But my children, because they were Parrs, would have been, *are* rich. Maybe my poor little children died, ran away, maybe she put them in an orphanage – *I* don't know. Or' – her voice suddenly changed totally, becoming dreamy, 'Or perhaps these are my children after all. Perhaps I'm imagining it all, after all I've been through. Miss Shore, this is just what I've come all the way from Scotland to beg you to find out.'

It was an extraordinary story. Jemima's original impulse had been to give Mrs Catharine Parr a cup of coffee and send her gently on her way. Now the overriding curiosity which was definitely her strongest attribute would not let her be. The appeals of the public to Jemima Shore Investigator certainly fell on compassionate ears; but they also fell on very inquisitive ones. In this instance she felt she owed it to the forces of common sense to point out first to Mrs Parr that lawyers could investigate such matters far more efficiently than she. To this Mrs Parr answered quite reasonably that lawyers would take an age, as they always did:

'And in the meantime what would happen to me and the children? We'd be getting to know each other, getting fond of each other. No, Miss Shore, *you* can settle it. I know you can. Then we can all get on with our lives for better or for worse.'

Then Jemima caved in and acceded to Mrs Parr's request.

It was in this way, for better or for worse as Mrs Parr had put it, that Jemima Shore Investigator found herself the following night taking the sleeper back to Inverness. The sleeping-car attendant recognised Mrs Parr quite merrily:

'Why it's you again, Mrs Parr. You'll keep British Rail in business with your travelling.' Then of course he recognised Jemima Shore with even greater delight. Later, taking her ticket, he was with difficulty restrained from confiding to her his full and rich life story which he was convinced would make an excellent television documentary. Staved off, he contented himself with approving Jemima's modest order of late-night tea.

'You're not like your friend, then, Mrs Parr . . .' he made a significant drinking gesture. 'The trouble I had with her going north the first time. Crying, and crying and disturbing all the passengers. However she was better the second time, and mebbe now you'll have a good influence on her, Miss Shore. I'll be seeing her now and asking her if this time she'll have a late-night cup of tea.' He bustled off, leaving Jemima faintly disquieted. She hoped that Mrs Parr had no drink aboard. The north of Scotland with an alcoholic, probably a fantasist into the bargain . . .

Morning found her in a more robust mood. Which was fortunate since Jemima's first sight of Kildrum Lodge, standing on the edge of a dark, seemingly endless loch, shut in by mountains, was once again disquieting. It was difficult for her to believe that Zillah could have brought the children to such a place out of sheer love for Scottish scenery and country pursuits such as fishing, swimming and walking. The situation of the lodge itself even for Scotland was so extremely isolated. Nor was the glen which led up to the lodge notably beautiful. A general lack of colour except blackness, in the water, reflected from the skies, made it in fact peculiarly depressing. There was a lack of vegetation even on the lower slopes of the mountains, which slid down straight into the loch. The single track road was bumpy and made of stones. It was difficult to imagine that much traffic passed that way. One could imagine a woman with something to hide – two children perhaps? – seeking out such a location, but not a warm comforting body hoping to cheer up her charges after the sudden death of their father.

The notion of Zillah's sinister purpose, far-fetched in London, suddenly seemed horribly plausible. And this was the loch, the very loch, in which Zillah herself had drowned. No, Kildrum to Jemima Shore did not have the air of a happy uncomplicated place. She looked across at Mrs Parr, in the passenger seat of the hired car. Mrs Parr looked pale. Whether she had passed the night consuming further bottles of wine or was merely dreading the next confrontation with the Parr children, the hands with which she was trying to light a cigarette were shaking. Jemima felt once more extremely sorry for her and glad that she had come to Kildrum.

They approached the lodge. It was surrounded by banks of dark green rhododendrons, growing unrestrained, which did nothing to cheer the surroundings. There was no other garden, only rough grass going down to the loch. The large windows of the lodge looked blank and unwelcoming. As Jemima drove slowly up the stony road, the front door opened and something white was glimpsed within. It was eerily quiet once the car's engine had stopped. Then the door opened further and the flash of white proved to be a girl wearing jeans and a blue jersey. She had extremely fair, almost lint-white hair, plaited. For a girl of eight she was quite well-built, even stocky.

'Tamsin,' said Mrs Parr. She pronounced the name as though for Jemima's benefit; but it was once again disquieting that she made no move towards the child. The interior of the house, like the glen itself and the mountains, was dark. Most of the paintwork was brown and the chintz curtains were patterned in a depressing brown and green. Nevertheless, some energy had obviously been spent recently in making it cosy. There were cheerful traces of childish occupation, books, a bright red anorak, shiny blue gumboots. Pot plants and an arrangement of leaves bore witness to the presence of a domestic spirit in the house – once upon a time.

In the large kitchen at the back of the house where Jemima insisted on repairing for coffee there was also an unmistakable trace of modern civilisation in the shape of a television set. There was a telephone too – but that was black and ancient-looking. Tamsin went with them, still silent. In the kitchen they were immediately joined by Tara, equally silent, equally blonde.

The two sisters stared warily at the women before them as if they were intruders. Which in a sense, thought Jemima, we are. Her eyes caught and held by the two striking flaxen heads, she recalled Mrs Parr's words concerning Zillah's nephew and niece: 'Quite fair too then, but not as fair as Zillah and not as fair as my children . . .' Could children actually become fairer as the years went by? Impossible. No one became fairer with time except out of a bottle. Even these children's hair was darkening slightly at the roots. Jemima felt that she had a first very positive clue that the Parr children were exactly what they purported to be. She was so relieved that a feeling of bonhomie seized her. She smiled warmly at the children and extended her hand.

'I'm Jemima Shore —'

'Investigator!' completed Tamsin triumphantly. And

from her back she produced a large placard on which the cheering words: 'Welcome Jemima Shaw Investogater' were carefully inscribed in a variety of lurid pentel colours.

'I did it,' exclaimed Tara.

'I did the spelling,' said Tamsin proudly.

Jemima decided it would be tactful to congratulate her on it. At least fame on the box granted you a kind of passport to instant friendship, whatever the circumstances. In the kitchen too was another figure prepared to be an instant friend: Mrs Elspeth Maxwell, caretaker of the lodge and since the death of Zillah, *in loco parentis* to the Parr children. Elspeth Maxwell, as Jemima quickly appreciated, was a woman of uncertain age but certain garrulity. Instinctively she summed people up as they would make good or bad subjects for an interview. Mrs Parr, madness and melodrama and all, would not in the end make good television. She was perhaps too obsessional at centre. But Elspeth Maxwell, under her flow of anecdote, might give you just that line or vital piece of information you needed to illuminate a whole topic. Jemima decided to cultivate her; whatever the cost in listening to a load of irrelevant gossip.

As a matter of fact Elspeth Maxwell needed about as much cultivation as the rhododendrons growing wild outside the house. During the next few days, Jemima found that her great problem consisted in getting away from Elspeth Maxwell, occupying the kitchen, and into the children's playroom. Mrs Parr spent most of the time in her bedroom. Her public excuse was that she wanted to let Jemima get on with her task, which had been described to Tamsin and Tara as investigation for a programme about children living in the Highlands. Privately she told Jemima that she wanted to keep clear of emotional involvement with the children 'until I'm *sure*. One way or the other.' Jemima thought there might be a third reason: that Mrs Parr wanted to consume at leisure her daily ration of cheap red wine. The pile of empty bottles on the rubbish dump behind the rhododendrons continued to grow and there was a smell of drink upstairs emanating from Mrs Parr's bedroom. Whenever Mrs Parr chose to empty an ash-tray it was overflowing. On one occasion Jemima tried the door. It was locked. After a moment Mrs Parr called out in a muffled voice:

'Go away. I'm resting.'

It was conclusive evidence of Mrs Parr's addiction that no drink was visible in the rest of the house. Jemima was never offered anything alcoholic, nor was any reference made to the subject. In her experience of alcoholics, that was far more damning than the sight of a rapidly diminishing sherry bottle in the sitting-room.

Elspeth on the subject of the children was interminable:

'Ach, the poor wee things! Terrible for them, now, wasn't it? Their mother drowned before their very eyes. What a tragedy. Here in Kildrum.'

'Step-mother,' corrected Jemima. Elspeth swept on. But the tale was indeed a tragic one, whichever way you looked at it.

'A fearful accident indeed. Though there's other people been drowned in the loch, you know, it's the weeds, those weeds pull you down, right to the bottom. And it's one of the deepest lochs in the Highlands, deeper than Loch Ness, nearly as deep as Loch Morar, did you know that, Miss Shore? Then their father not so long dead, I believe, and this lady coming, their real mother, all on top of it. Then you, so famous, from television . . .'

The trouble was that, for all her verbiage, Elspeth Maxwell could not really tell Jemima anything much about Zillah herself, still less about her relationship with Tamsin and Tara. It was Elspeth who had had the task of sorting out Zillah's effects and putting them into suitcases, still lying upstairs while some sort of decision was reached as to what to do with them. These Jemima made a mental note to examine as soon as possible. Otherwise Elspeth had seen absolutely nothing of Zillah during her sojourn at Kildrum Lodge.

'She wanted no help, she told the Estate Office. She could perfectly well take care of the lodge, she said, and the children. She was used to it. And the cooking. She wanted peace and quiet, she said, and to fish and walk and swim and go out in the boat – ' Elspeth stopped. 'Ah well, poor lady. But she certainly kept herself very close, herself and the children. No one knew her in Kildrum. Polite, mind you, a very polite lady, they said at the Estate Office, wrote very polite letters and notes. But very close.'

And the children? The verdict was more or less the same. Yes, they had certainly seemed very fond of Zillah whenever glimpsed in Kildrum. But generally shy, reserved. And once again polite. Elspeth could only recall one conversation of any moment before Zillah's death out of a series of little interchanges and that was when Tamsin, in Kildrum Post Office, referred to the impending arrival of Mrs Parr. Elspeth, out of motherly sympathy for their apparent loneliness, had invited Tamsin and Tara to tea with her in the village. Tamsin had refused:

'A lady's coming from London to see us. She says she's our Mummy. But Tara and me think Zillah is our Mummy.' It was, remarked Elspeth, an unusual burst of confidence from Tamsin. She had put it down to Tamsin's distaste at the thought of the arrival of 'the lady from London' – while of course becoming madly curious about Tamsin's family history. As a result of a 'wee discussion' of the subject in her own home, she had actually put two and two together and realised that these were the once famous Parr children. Elspeth, even in Kildrum, had naturally had strong views on *that* subject. How she would now have adored some contact with the household at Kildrum Lodge! But that was politely but steadfastly denied her. Until Zillah's death, ironically enough, brought to Elspeth exactly that involvement she had so long desired.

'I did think: mebbe she has something to hide, and my brother-in-law, Johnnie Maxwell, the ghillie, he thought mebbe the same. Keeping herself so much to herself. But all along, I dare say it was just the fear of the other mother, that one,' Elspeth rolled her eyes to the ceiling where Mrs Parr might be supposed to lie 'resting' in her bedroom. 'Fear of her finding the children. Ah well, it's difficult to judge her altogether wrong. If you know what I mean. The dreadful case. All that publicity.'

But Elspeth looked as if she would readily re-hash every detail of the case of the Parr children, despite the publicity, for Jemima's benefit.

None of this was particularly helpful. Nor did

inspection of Zillah's personal belongings, neatly sorted by Elspeth, bring any reward. It was not that Jemima expected to find a signed confession: 'Tamsin and Tara are imposters. They are the children of my sister . . .' Indeed, she was coming more and more to the conclusion that Mrs Parr's mad suspicions were the product of a mind disordered by alcohol. But Jemima did hope to provide herself with some kind of additional picture of the dead woman, other than the malevolent reports of the first Mrs Parr, and the secondhand gossip of Elspeth Maxwell. All she discovered was that Zillah, like Jemima herself, had an inordinate fondness for the colour beige, presumably for the same reason, to complement her fair colouring; and like a good many other English women, but unlike Jemima, bought her underclothes at Marks & Spencer's (Jemima patronised Janet Reger). Jemima did not like to speculate where and when Mrs Parr might have last bought her underclothes.

There were various photographs of Tamsin and Tara but none pre-dating Scotland. There were also some photographs of Zillah's sister Kitty; she did look vaguely like Mrs Parr, Jemima noticed, but no more than that; their features were different; it was a question of physical type rather than strict resemblance. There were no photographs of Kitty's children. Was that sinister? Conceivably. Or maybe she had merely lost touch with them. Was it also sinister that Zillah had not preserved photographs of Tamsin and Tara in Sussex? Once again: conceivably. On the other hand Zillah might have packed away all her Sussex mementoes (there were no photographs of Mr Parr either). Perhaps she came into that category of grief-stricken person who prefers not to be reminded of the past.

From the Estate Office Jemima drew another blank. Major Maclachlan, who had had the unenviable task of identifying Zillah's body, was polite enough, particularly at the thought of a television programme popularising his corner of the Highlands. But he added very little to the public portrait of a woman whose chief characteristic was her reserve and determination to guard her privacy – her own and that of the children. Her love of country sports, especially fishing, had however impressed him: Major Maclachlan clearly found it unjust that someone with such admirable tastes should have perished as a result of them.

Only Johnnie Maxwell, Elspeth's brother-in-law who was in charge of fishing on the loch, contributed anything at all to her enquiries. For it was Johnnie Maxwell who had been the principal witness at the inquest, having watched the whole drowning from the bank of the loch. To the newspaper account of the tragedy, which Jemima had read, he added some ghoulish details of the pathetic cries of the 'wee girl', unable to save Zillah. The children had believed themselves alone on the loch. In vain Johnnie had called to them to throw in the oar. Tamsin had merely screamed and screamed, oar in hand, Tara had sat quite still and silent, as though dumbstruck in horror. In their distress they did not seem to understand, or perhaps they could not hear him.

Altogether it was a most unfortunate, if not unparalleled accident. One moment Zillah was casting confidently ('Aye, she was a grand fisherwoman, the poor lady, more's the pity'). The next moment she had overbalanced and fallen in the water. There was no one else in the boat except the two children, and no one else to be seen on the shores of the loch except Johnnie. By the time he got his own boat to the children, Zillah had completely vanished and Tamsin was in hysterics, Tara quite mute. Helpers came up from the Estate. They did not find the body till the next morning, when it surfaced in the thick reeds at the shore. There were some bruises on it, but nothing that could not be explained by a fall from the boat and prolonged immersion.

That left the children. Jemima felt she owed it to Mrs Parr to cross-examine them a little on their background. Confident that she would turn up nothing to their disadvantage, she could at least reassure Mrs Parr thoroughly as a result. After that she trusted that her eccentric new contact would settle into normal family life or the nearest approximation to it she could manage. Yes, the gentle, efficient cross-examination of Tamsin and Tara would be her final task and then Jemima Shore, Investigator, would depart for London, having closed the case of the Parr children once and for all.

But it did not work out quite like that.

The children, in their different ways, were friendly enough. Tamsin was even quite talkative once her initial shyness wore off. She had a way of tossing her head so that the blonde pigtails shook, like a show pony shaking its mane. Tara was more silent and physically frailer. But she sprang into life whenever Tamsin felt the need to contradict her, as being her elder and better. Arguing with Tamsin made even Tara quite animated. You could imagine both settling down quite easily once the double shock of Zillah's death and their real mother's arrival had been assimilated.

Nevertheless, something was odd. It was instinct not reason that guided her. Reason told her that Mrs Parr's accusations were absurd. But then nagging instinct would not leave her in peace. She had interviewed too many subjects, she told herself, to be wrong now. . . . Then reason reasserted itself once more, with the aid of the children's perfectly straightforward account of their past. They referred quite naturally to their life in Sussex.

'We went to a horrid school with nasty rough boys —' began Tara.

'It was a *lovely* school,' interrupted Tamsin. 'I played football with the boys in my break. Silly little girls like Tara couldn't do that.' All of this accorded with the facts given by the lawyer: how the girls had attended the local primary school which was fine for the tomboy Tamsin, not so good for the shrinking Tara. They would have gone to the reputedly excellent school in Kildrum when the Scottish term started had it not been for the death of Zillah.

Nevertheless, something was odd, strange, not quite right.

Was it perhaps the fact that the girls never seemed to talk amongst themselves which disconcerted her? After considerable pondering on the subject, Jemima decided that the silence of Tamsin and Tara when alone – no happy or unhappy sounds coming out of their playroom or bedroom – was the most upsetting thing about them. Even the sporadic quarrelling brought on by Tamsin's bossiness ceased. Yet Jemima's experience of children was that sporadic quarrels in front of grown-ups turned to outright war in private. But she was here as an investigator not as a child analyst (who might or might not have to follow later). Who was she to estimate the shock effect of Zillah's death, in front of their own eyes? Perhaps their confidence had been so rocked by the boating accident that they literally could not speak when alone. It was, when all was said and done, a minor matter compared to the evident correlation of the girls' stories with their proper background.

And yet . . . There was after all the whole question of Zillah's absent nieces. Now, was that satisfactorily dealt with or not? Torn between reason and instinct Jemima found it impossible to make up her mind. She naturally raised the subject, in what she hoped to be a discreet manner. For once it was Tara who answered first:

'Oh, no, we never see them. You see they went to America for Christmas and they didn't come back.' She sounded quite blithe.

'Canada, silly,' said Tamsin.

'Same thing.'

'It's not, silly.'

'It is —'

'Christmas?' pressed Jemima.

'They went for a Christmas holiday to America. Aunt Kitty took them and they never came back.'

'They went *forever*,' interrupted Tamsin fiercely. 'They went to Canada and they went *forever*. That's what Zillah said. Aunt Kitty doesn't even send us Christmas cards.' Were the answers, as corrected by Tamsin, a little too pat?

A thought struck Jemima. Later that night she consulted Mrs Parr. If Zillah's sister had been her next of kin, had not the lawyers tried to contact her on Zillah's death? Slightly reluctantly Mrs Parr admitted that the lawyers had tried and so far failed to do so. 'Oddly enough it seemed I was Zillah's next of kin after Kitty,' she added. But Kitty had emigrated to Canada (yes, Canada, Tamsin as usual was right) several years earlier and was at present address unknown. And she was supposed to have taken her two daughters with her.

It was at this point Jemima decided to throw in her hand. In her opinion the investigation was over, the Parr children had emerged with flying colours, and as for their slight oddity, well, that was really only to be expected, wasn't it? Under the circumstances. It was time to get back to Megalith Television and the autumn series. She communicated her decision to Mrs Parr, before nagging instinct could resurrect its tiresome head again.

'You don't feel it then, Jemima?' Mrs Parr sounded for the first time neither vehement nor dreamy but dimly hopeful. 'You don't sense something about them? That they're hiding something? Something strange, unnatural . . .'

'No, I do not,' answered Jemima Shore firmly.

'And if I were you, Catharine' – they had evolved a spurious but convenient intimacy during their days in the lonely lodge – 'I would put all such thoughts behind you. See them as part of the ordeal you have suffered, a kind of long illness. Now you must convalesce and recover. And help your children, your own children, to recover too.' It was Jemima Shore at her most bracing. She hoped passionately not so much that she was correct about the children – with every minute she was more convinced of the rightness of reason, the falseness of instinct – but that Mrs Parr would now feel able to welcome them to her somewhat neurotic bosom. She might even give up drink.

Afterwards Jemima would always wonder whether these were the fatal words which turned the case of the Parr children from a mystery into a tragedy. Could she even then have realised or guessed the truth? The silence of the little girls together: did she gloss too easily over that? But by that time it was too late.

As it was, immediately Jemima had spoken, Mrs Parr seemed to justify her decision in the most warming way. She positively glowed with delight. For a moment Jemima had a glimpse of the dashing young woman who had thrown up her comfortable home to go off with the raggle-taggle-gypsies seven years before. This ardent and presumably attractive creature had been singularly lacking in the Mrs Parr she knew. She referred to herself now as 'lucky Catharine Parr', no longer the wretched Queen who lost her head. Jemima was reminded for an instant of one of the few subjects who had bested her in argument on television, a mother opposing organised schooling, like Catharine Parr a Bohemian. There was the same air of elation. The quick change was rather worrying. Lucky Catharine Parr: Jemima only hoped that she would be third time lucky as the sleeping car attendant had suggested. It rather depended on what stability she could show as a mother.

'I promise you,' cried Mrs Parr, interrupting a new train of thought, 'I give you my word. I'll never ever think about the past again. I'll look after them to my dying day. I'll give them all the love in the world, all the love they've missed all these years. Miss Shore, Jemima, I told you I trusted you. You've done all I asked you to do. Thank you, thank you.'

The next morning dawned horribly wet. It was an added reason for Jemima to be glad to be leaving Kildrum Lodge. A damp Scottish August did not commend itself to her. With nothing further to do, the dripping rhododendrons surrounding the lodge were beginning to depress her spirits. Rain sheeted down on the loch, making even a brisk walk seem impractical. With the children still silent in their playroom and Mrs Parr still lurking upstairs for the kind of late morning rise she favoured, Jemima decided to make her farewell to Elspeth Maxwell in the kitchen.

She was quickly trapped in the flood of Elspeth's reflections, compared to which the rain outside seemed suddenly mild in contrast. Television intrigued Elspeth Maxwell in general, and Jemima, its incarnation, intrigued her in particular. She was avid for every detail of Jemima's appearances on the box, how many new clothes she needed, television make-up and so forth. On the subject of hair, she first admired the colour of Jemima's corn-coloured locks, then asked how often she had to have a shampoo, and finally enquired with a touch of acerbity:

'You'll not be putting anything on, then? I'm meaning the colour, what a beautiful bright colour your hair is, Miss Shore. You'll not be using one of those little bottles?'

Jemima smilingly denied it. 'I'm lucky.' She wasn't sure

whether Elspeth believed her. After a bit Elspeth continued: 'Not like that poor lady.' She seemed obsessed with the subject. Was she thinking of dyeing her own hair? 'The late Mrs Parr, I mean, when I cleared out her things, I found plenty of bottles, different colours, dark and fair, as though she'd been making a wee experiment. And she had lovely fair hair herself, or so they said, Johnnie and the men, when they took her out of the water. Just like the children. Look —' Elspeth suddenly produced two bottles from out of the kitchen cupboard. One was called Goldilocks and the other Brown Leaf. Jemima thought her guess was right. Elspeth was contemplating her own wee experiment.

'I'm thinking you'll not be needing this on your *natural* fair hair.' There was a faint ironic emphasis in Elspeth's tone. 'And Tamsin and Tara, they'll have lovely hair to when they grow up. They won't need Goldilocks or such things. And who would want Brown Leaf anyway with lovely fair hair like theirs? And yours. Brown Leaf would only hide the colour.' Elspeth put the bottles back in the cupboard as though that settled the matter.

Irritated by her malice – there was nothing wrong with dyeing one's hair but Jemima just did not happen to do it – Jemima abandoned Elspeth and the kitchen for the nursery. Nevertheless, Elspeth's words continued to ring in her head. That and another remark she could not forget. Tamsin and Tara were both reading quietly, lying on their tummies on the floor. Tamsin looked up and smiled.

'When will the programme be, Miss Shore?' she asked brightly. 'When will you come back and film us? Oh, I'm so sad you're going away.'

Jemima was standing by the mantelpiece. It had a large mirror over it, which gave some light to the dark room. In the mirror she gazed back into the room, at the striking blonde heads of the two children lying on the floor. It was of course a mirror image, reversed. The sight was symbolical. It was as though for the first time she was seeing the case of the Parr children turned inside out, reversed, black white, dark fair . . . Lucky children with their mother restored to them. A mother who drank and smoked and was totally undomesticated. But was still their mother. Zillah had done none of these things – but she had done worse: she had tried to keep the children from the mother who bore them. Lucky. Third time lucky.

Jemima stood absolutely still. Behind her back Tamsin smiled again that happy innocent smile. Tara was smiling too.

'Oh yes, Miss Shore,' she echoed, 'I'm so sad you're going away.' For once Tara was in total agreement with her sister. And in the mirror Jemima saw both girls dissolve into soundless giggles, hands over the mouth to stifle the noise. She continued to stare at the children's blonde heads.

With sudden horrible clarity, Jemima knew that she was wrong, had been wrong all along. She would have to tell the woman resting upstairs that the children were not after all her own. A remark that had long haunted her came to the front of her mind. Catharine Parr: 'Just like the wretched Queen who lost her head, and I'm just as wretched.' And now she knew why it had haunted her. Catharine Parr had not been executed by Henry VIII, but she had been childless by him. Now she would have to break it to Mrs Parr that she too was childless. Would be childless in the future.

It had to be done. There was such a thing as truth. Truth – and justice. But first, however dreadfully, she had to confront the children with what they had done. She had to make them admit it.

Wheeling round, she said as calmly as possible to the little girls: 'I'm just going to drive to the telephone box to arrange with my secretary about my return. This telephone is out of order with the storm last night.' She thought she could trust Tamsin to accept that story. Then Jemima added:

'And when I come back, we'll go out in the boat. Will you tell your – ' she paused in spite of herself – 'Will you tell your Mummy that?'

The children were not smiling now.

'The boat!' exclaimed Tamsin. 'But our Mummy can't swim. She told us.' She sounded tearful. 'She told us not to go in the boat, and anyway we don't want to. She told us we'd never ever have to go in the boat again.'

'Oh don't make us go in the horrid boat, Miss Shore,' Tara's eyes were wide with apprehension. 'Please don't. We can't swim. We never learnt yet.'

'I can swim,' replied Jemima, 'I'm a strong swimmer. Will you give your Mummy my message?'

When Jemima got back, Mrs Parr was standing with Tamsin and Tara by the door of the lodge, holding their hands (the first time Jemima had glimpsed any sign of physical affection in her). She was looking extremely distressed. She was wearing a filthy torn mackintosh in which she had first appeared at Jemima's flat. Her appearance, which had improved slightly over the last few days, was as unkempt and desperate as it had been on that weird occasion.

'Miss Shore, you mustn't do this,' she cried, the moment Jemima was out of the car. 'We can't go out in the boat. It's terrible for the children after – after what happened. Besides, I can't swim —'

'I'm sorry, Catharine,' was all Jemima said. She did not relish what she had to do.

Perhaps because she was childless herself, Jemima Shore believed passionately that young children were basically innocent whatever they did. After all, had the Parr children ever really had a chance in life since its disturbed beginnings? And now she, the alleged protector of the weak, the compassionate social campaigner, was going to administer the *coup de grâce*. She wished profoundly that she had not answered the bell to Mrs Parr that fatal Sunday morning.

The rain had stopped. The weather was clearing above the mountains in the west although the sky over the loch remained sullen. In silence the little party entered the rowing boat and Jemima pushed off from the soft ground of the foreshore.

'Come on, Tamsin, sit by me. Row like you did that afternoon with Zillah.'

Mrs Parr gave one more cry:

'Miss Shore! No.' Then she relapsed with a sort of groan into the seat of the stern of the boat. Tara sat beside her, facing Jemima and Tamsin.

After a while Jemima rested on her oar. They were near

the middle of the loch. The lodge looked small and far away, the mountains behind less menacing. Following the rain the temperature had risen. Presently the sun came out. It was quite humid. Flies buzzed round Jemima's head and the children. Soon the midges would come to torture them. The water had a forbidding look: she could see thick green weeds floating just beneath the surface. An occasional fish rose and broke the black surface. No one was visible amongst the reeds. They were, the silent boatload, alone on the loch.

Or perhaps they were not alone. Perhaps Johnnie Maxwell the ghillie was somewhere amid the sedge, at his work. If so he would have seen yet another macabre sight on Loch Drum. He would have seen Jemima Shore, her red-gold hair illuminated by the sunlight, lean forward and grab Tara from her seat. He would have seen her hurl the little girl quite far into the lake, like some human Excalibur. He would have heard the loud splash, seen the spreading circles on the black water. Then he would surely, even at the edge of the loch – for the air was very still after the rain – have heard Tara's cries. But even if Johnnie Maxwell had been watching, he would have been once again helpless to have saved the drowning person.

Mrs Parr gave a single loud scream and stood up at the stern of the boat. Jemima Shore sat grimly still, like a figure of vengeance. Tamsin got to her feet, wielded her oar and tried in vain to reach out to the child, splashing hopelessly now on, now under the surface of the loch. Jemima Shore continued to sit still.

When a child's voice was heard, half choking with water:

'Zillah, save me! Zillah!'

It seemed as though the woman standing at the stern of the boat would never move. Suddenly, uncontrollably, she tore off her white mackintosh. And without further hesitation, she made a perfect racing dive onto the surface of the loch. Minutes later Tara, still sobbing and spluttering, but alive, was safely out of the water. Then for the first time since she had thrown Tara into the loch, Jemima Shore made a move – to pull the woman who had called herself Mrs Catharine Parr back into the boat again.

'The police are coming, of course,' said Jemima. They were back at the house;. 'You killed her, didn't you?'

Tamsin and Tara, in dry clothes, had been sent out to play among the rhododendrons which served for a garden. The sun was gaining intensity. The loch had moved from black to grey to slate blue. Tara was bewildered. Tamsin was angry.

'Goodbye, *Mummy*,' she said fiercely to Zillah.

'Don't make her pretend any longer,' Jemima too appealed to Zillah. And to Tamsin: 'I know you see. I've known for some time.'

Tamsin then turned to her sister: 'Baby. You gave it away. You promised never to call her Zillah. Now they'll come and take Zillah away. I won't ever speak to you again.' And Tamsin ran off into the dark shrubberies.

Zillah Parr, wearing some of her own clothes fished out of Elspeth's packages, was sitting with Jemima by the playroom fire. She looked neat and clean and reassuring, a child's dream mother, as she must always have looked during the last seven years. Until she deliberately assumed the messy run-down identity of Mrs Parr that is. How this paragon must have hated to dirty her fingernails! Jemima noticed that she had seized the opportunity to scrub them vigorously while she was upstairs in the bathroom changing.

Now the mirror reflected a perfectly composed woman, legs in nice shoes, neatly crossed, sipping the glass of whisky which Jemima had given her.

'Why not?' said Zillah coolly. 'I never drink you know, normally. Unlike *her*. Nor do I smoke. I find both things quite disgusting. As for pretending to be drunk! I used to pour all those wine bottles down the sink. But I never found a good way of producing cigarette stubs without smoking. Ugh, the smell. I never got used to it. But I feel I may need the whisky this afternoon.'

Silence fell between them. Then Zillah said quite conversationally: 'By the way, how did you know?'

'A historical inaccuracy was your first mistake,' replied Jemima. They might have been analysing a game of bridge. 'It always struck me as odd that a woman called Catharine Parr, and an educated woman to boot, would not have known the simple facts of her namesake's life. It was Catharine Howard by the way who lost her head, not Catharine Parr.'

'Oh really.' Zillah sounded quite uninterested. 'Well, I never had any education. I saw no use for it in my work, either.'

'But you made other mistakes. The sleeping-car attendant: that was a risk to take. He recognised you because of all the drinking. He spoke of you being third time lucky, and at first I thought he meant your quick journey up and down from London to Inverness and back. But then I realised that he meant that this was your third journey *northwards*. He spoke of you "going north" the second time and how you weren't so drunk as the first time. She went up first, didn't she? You killed her. Then faked your own death, and somehow got down to London secretly, perhaps from another station. Then up and down again under the name of Catharine Parr.'

'That was unlucky.' Zillah agreed. 'Of course I didn't know that he'd met the real Catharine Parr when I travelled up under her name the first time. I might have been more careful.'

'In the end it was a remark of Elspeth Maxwell's which gave me the clue. That, and your expression.'

'That woman! She talks far too much,' said Zillah with a frown.

'The dyes: she showed me the various dyes you had used, I suppose to dye Mrs Parr's hair blonde and darken your own.'

'She dyed her own hair,' Zillah sounded positively complacent. 'I've always been good at getting people to do things. I baited her. Pointed out how well I'd taken care of myself, my hair still blonde and thick, and what a mess she looked. Why, I looked more like the children's mother than she did. I knew that would get her. We'd once been awfully alike, you see, at least to look at. You never guessed that, did you? Kitty never really looked much like her, different nose, different-shaped face. But as girls, Catharine and I were often mistaken for each other. It even happened once or twice when I was working for her. And how patronising she was about it. "Oh no, that was just Zillah," she used to say with that awful laugh of hers when she's been drinking. "Local saint and poor relation." I think that's why he – the children's father – first fell in love with me. I was like her but not like.' Zillah hesitated and then went on more briskly.

'I showed her the bottle of Goldilocks, pretended I used it myself and she grabbed it. "Now we'll see who the children's real mother is," she said, when she'd finished.'

'The bottle did fool me at first,' admitted Jemima. 'I thought it must be connected somehow with the children's hair. Then Elspeth gave me the key when she wondered aloud who would ever use Brown Leaf if they had fair hair: "It would only hide the colour." ' She paused. 'So you killed her, blonde hair and all,' she said.

'Yes, I killed her,' Zillah was still absolutely composed. She seemed to have no shame or even fear. 'I drowned her. She was going to take the children away. I found out that she couldn't swim, took her out in the boat in the morning when I knew Johnnie Maxwell wasn't around. Then I let her drown. I would have done anything to keep the children,' she added.

'I told the children that she'd gone away,' she went on. 'That horrid drunken old tramp. Naturally I didn't tell them I'd killed her. I just said that we would play a game. A game in which I would pretend to fall into the lake and be drowned. Then I would dress up in her old clothes and pretend to *be* her. And they must treat me just as if I *was* her, all cold and distant. They must never hug me as if I was Zillah. And if they played it properly, if they never talked about it to anyone, not even each other when they were alone, the horrid mother would never come back. And then I could be their proper mother. Just as they had always wanted. Zillah, they used to say with their arms round me, we love you so much, won't you be our Mummy forever?' Her voice became dreamy and for a moment Zillah was reminded of the person she had known as Catharine Parr. 'I couldn't have any children of my own, you see; I had to have an operation when I was quite young. Wasn't it unfair? That she could have them, who was such a terrible mother, and I couldn't. All my life I've always loved other people's children. My sister's. Then his children.'

'It was the children all along, wasn't it? Not the money. The Parr Trust: that was a red herring.'

'The money!' exclaimed Zillah. Her voice was full of contempt. 'The Parr Trust meant nothing to me. It was an encumbrance if anything. Little children don't need money: they need love and that's exactly what I gave to them. And she would have taken them away, the selfish good-for-nothing tramp that she was, that's what she threatened to do, take them away, and never let me see them again. She said in her drunken way, laughing and drinking together: "This time, my fine cousin Zillah, the law will be on my side." So I killed her. And so I defeated her. Just as I defeated her the last time when she tried to take the children away from me in court.'

'And from their father,' interposed Jemima.

'The judge knew a real motherly woman when he saw one,' Zillah went on as though she had not heard. 'He said so in court for all the world to hear. And he was right, wasn't he? Seven years she left them. Not a card. Not a present. And then thinking she could come back, just like that, because their father was dead, and claim them. All for an accident of birth. She was nothing to them, *nothing*, and I was everything.'

And Jemima herself? Her mission?

'Oh yes, I got you here deliberately. To test the children. I was quite confident, you see. I knew they would fool you. But I wanted them to know the sort of questions they would be asked – by lawyers, even perhaps the Press. I used to watch you on television,' she added with a trace of contempt. 'I fooled that judge. He never knew about their father and me. I enjoy fooling people when it's necessary. I knew I could fool you.'

'But you didn't,' said Jemima Shore coldly. She did not like the idea of being fooled. 'There was one more clue. An expression. The expression of triumph on your face when I told you I was satisfied about the children and was going back to London. You dropped your guard for a moment. It reminded me of a woman who had once scored over me on television. I didn't forget that.' She added, 'Besides, you would never have got away with it.'

But privately she thought that if Zillah Parr had not displayed her arrogance by sending for Jemima Shore, Investigator, as a guinea pig she might well have done so. After all, no one had seen Catharine Parr for seven years; bitterly she had cut herself off completely from all her old friends when she went to Ireland. Zillah had also led a deliberately isolated life after her husband's death; in her case she had hoped to elude the children's mother should she ever reappear. Zillah's sister had vanished to Canada. Elspeth Maxwell had been held at arm's length, as had the inhabitants of Kildrum. Johnnie Maxwell had met Zillah once but there was no need for him to meet the false Mrs Parr, who so much disliked fishing.

The two women were much of an age and their physical resemblance in youth, striking: that resemblance which Zillah suggested had first attracted Mr Parr towards her. Only the hair had to be remedied, since Catharine's untended hair had darkened so much with the passing of the years. As for the corpse, the Parr family lawyer, whom Zillah had met face to face at the time of her husband's death, was, she knew, on holiday in Greece. It was not difficult to fake a resemblance sufficient to make Major Maclachlan at the Estate Office identify the body as that of Zillah Parr. The truth was so very bizarre: he was hardly likely to suspect it. He would be expecting to see the corpse of Zillah Parr, following Johnnie's account, and the corpse of Zillah Parr, bedraggled by the loch, he would duly see.

The unkempt air of a tramp was remarkably easy to assume: it was largely a matter of externals. After a while the new Mrs Catharine Parr would have discreetly improved her appearance. She would have left Kildrum – who would have blamed her? – and started a new life elsewhere. A new life with the children. Her own children: at last.

As all this was passing through Jemima's head, suddenly Zillah's control snapped. She started to cry: 'My children, my children. Not hers, *Mine* —' And she was still crying when the police car came up the rough drive, and tall men with black and white check bands round their hats took her away. First they had read her the warrant: 'Mrs Zillah Parr, I charge you with the murder of Mrs Catharine Parr, on or about the morning of August 6 . . . at Kildrum Lodge, Inverness-shire.'

As the police car vanished from sight down the lonely valley, Tara came out of the rhododendrons and put her hand in Jemima's. There was no sign of Tamsin.

'She will come back, Miss Shore, won't she?' she said anxiously. 'Zillah, I mean, not that Mummy. I didn't like that Mummy. She drank bottles all the time and shouted at us. She said rude words, words we're not allowed to say. I cried when she came and Tamsin hid. That Mummy even tried to hit me. But Zillah told us she would make the horrid Mummy go away. And she did. When will Zillah come back, Miss Shore?'

Holding Tara's hand, Jemima reflected sadly that the case of the Parr children was probably only just beginning.

ROMANCE 1988

Doris Lessing

Two young women sat on opposite sides of a table in the cafeteria in Terminal Three, Heathrow airport. They were in the raised part, which is like a little stage. Sybil had gone straight to this area though there were places empty in the lower, less emphasised, part of the room.

They were sisters, both large-boned, stocky, with broad sensible faces. But Sybil refused to be ordinary, wore dramatic makeup, short yellow hair, clothes you had to look at. She was a dazzler, like a pop star. No one would particularly notice Joan, and she sat admiring Sybil and giving London full credit, at least for this: they were from northern England, and they valued this sound inheritance, so much better than anything the frivolous and spoiled south could produce. They were in the old tradition of two sisters, the pretty one and the clever one, and so they had been cast in their childhoods – Joan, clever, and Sybil, pretty. But they were both clever attractive hard-working girls who pursued their chances with skill.

Joan was saying, 'But you're only twenty-two. I thought you were going to take your time?' She was the older sister, twenty-four.

Sybil said in her loud careless voice that everyone had to listen to, always, 'But my dear, I'll never find anyone like Oliver, I know that.'

Joan smiled. Deliberately. She raised her brows.

Sybil grinned at her, acknowledging the older sister act.

They did not need to hurry this conversation. Joan was

on her way to Bahrain where she had got herself a job as secretary in a part-American, part-English firm. She had just flown in from Yorkshire, and there were three hours before her flight out. Sybil had said that of course she would come out to Heathrow to be with her sister, no, it didn't matter, she just wouldn't go to work that day. She had arrived in London two years before and had at once taken possession of it, getting herself – God only knew how – a secondhand car, and she thought nothing of driving out to the airport at six in the morning or eleven at night to have a chat with friends who were always on their way through, or of dropping in on several parties in one night, in places as far apart as Greenwich and Chiswick. She had come to London as a secretary, but had decided that 'temping' was a better bet. Thus one sampled all kinds of different work, met a lot of different men, and when she was offered a job that suited her she would stay put. At least, that was what she had said until recently.

'You said all that about Geoff, remember,' said Joan, not unpleasantly, but putting the case.

'Oh *God*,' said Sybil, 'but I was only an infant then.'

'Eighteen,' said Joan.

'All right! Granted! And I know it doesn't sound likely, but we are made for each other, Oliver and I.'

'Has he said so?'

'I think we're in for it – marriage, kids, a mortgage, the lot.' The loud confident voice was attracting attention, and Joan was embarrassed. As she had been, all her life, by her sister.

She said in a pointedly low voice, 'Sybil, you told me it was all off with Oliver.'

'Yes, I know I did,' said Sybil loudly. 'He said he didn't want to marry again. He liked being free. And off he went. I didn't see him for months. He broke my heart. When he came after me again I said to him, You've broken my heart once, so this time you're going to have to make the running, I'm not coming after you. Not the way I did when I first met him,' she explained. And she cast a glance around to make sure her audience was still rapt.

Joan considered all this. Then she asked, 'When you're

married, are you going to travel abroad with him when he's on his trips?'

Oliver travelled a great deal for his firm, was more often away than in London.

'No. Oh well, I'll go with him sometimes, if it's somewhere interesting, but I'll make a home for him in London. No, I'm going to be a real wife,' she insisted, to her sister's quizzical smile.

'You always have to go to extremes.'

'What's extreme about that?'

'If you can't see it's over the top! Anyway, last time you said whenever he went abroad he took a different girl.'

'Yes, I know. He was in Rome last week and I knew he had slept with someone though he didn't say and I didn't ask. Because it was not my business . . .' Joan was looking so humorous that it was with an effect of shouting against noise that Sybil went on, '*Yes*. But then he confessed he had slept with someone and he felt guilty about it. Because of me. And I've been feeling guilty if I slept with anyone but him right from the very first time I slept with him.'

'Well,' sighed Joan, 'I suppose that's pretty conclusive.'

'Yes, I think it is. And what about you and Derek? Is he going to wait until you get back from Bahrain?'

'He says he will, but I have my doubts.'

They smiled at each other.

'Plenty of fish in the sea,' said Sybil.

'He's all right. But I reckon I'll have saved up thirty thousand out there, that is if I stick it out. There's nothing to spend anything on.'

'And then you'll be independent.'

'Yes. I'll buy a house the moment I get back.'

'Makes sense. And Oliver and I are looking for a house. We were looking last Sunday. It's fun looking at houses. There was one I think he would settle for, but I said to him, No, if we are going to be Upwardly Mobile, then let's *do* it. That house isn't good enough. You're doing better and better all the time, I said to him. Because he is. He's shooting up in his firm, and he gets more and more eligible every day.'

'You always did say you would marry for money.'

'Yes, I did. And I am. But I wouldn't marry him if I didn't feel like this about him.'

'But do you feel like this about him because he is so eligible?' enquired Joan, laughing.

'Probably. But what's the matter with that?'

'Would you marry him if he was poor?'

The sisters were now leaning forward, faces close, laughing and full of enjoyment.

'No, I wouldn't. I've got to have money. I know myself, don't I?'

'I hope you do,' said the older sister, suddenly sober.

Meanwhile people nearby were smiling at each other because of the two young adventurers, probably feeling that they ought to be shocked or something.

There was a pause, while they attended to coffee, croissants, fruit juice.

And then, suddenly, Sybil announced, 'And we are both going to have an AIDS test.' Now the people listening stopped smiling, though they were certainly attending. 'We both decided, at the same time. I mentioned it first, and found he had thought of it too. He slept around a lot after his divorce, and I have too, since I came to London. And you never know. But the trouble is, I'm going to have it done privately, because if it's on the National Health then it's in the records for everyone to see. Because then it would look as if you were worried.'

'And it's expensive.'

'Yes. Well, I can't afford it, I don't have the money, but Oliver can and he'll pay for me.'

Joan smiled. 'Certainly one way of making him responsible for you.'

'Yes, it is.'

'What will you do if either of you is positive?'

'Oh, I'm sure we won't be! We're both as hetero as they come. But you never know. We want to be on the safe side. No, we'll have the tests done and then we'll give each other our certificates.' Her face was soft and dreamy, full of love. For the first time she had forgotten her audience.

'Well,' said Joan, taking neat little sips of coffee, 'I suppose that's one way of doing it.'

'It means much more than an engagement ring, I mean, it's a real commitment.'

'And he is going to have to be faithful to you now, isn't he?'

'But I'll have to be faithful to him!'

Joan's face was suggesting this was not the same thing. Then she asked, teasing, 'Faithful for ever?'

'Yes . . . well . . . for as long as we can, anyway. We don't want to sleep with anyone else, not the way we feel now. What's the point of risking it, anyway?'

She glanced around, but her audience no longer attended to her. They were talking to each other. If this was their way of showing disapproval, then . . .

Two and a half hours to go.

Sybil raised her voice. 'We tried condoms, too, but God knows how people get them to work. We laughed so much that in the end we simply had to settle for going to sleep.'

'Shhhhh,' said Joan, in agony. 'Shhhhhh.'

'Why? What's the matter, no, let me tell you, if the safety of the nation is going to depend on condoms, then . . .'

At this point a young man who had been sitting near them, listening, got up because it was time for him to be off on his way to somewhere or other in the world. He tapped Sybil on the shoulder and said, 'If you can't get the hang of condoms, then just get in touch with me . . . no, no, any time, a pleasure!'

His words were far from an invitation, were more of a public rebuke, and on his face was the look that goes with someone taking it on himself to keep things in order. But from the door he sent them a glance and a grin and disappeared for ever with a wave. As for Joan and Sybil, they sat half turned to watch him go. They looked like a couple of teenagers, their hands half-covering scandalised and delighted smiles.

THE BUNTING AFFIRMS

H. R. F. Keating

The King came out of the Home Office into Whitehall at twenty minutes to eleven exactly. The year of Our Lord nineteen hundred and twenty. Maurice, from his place in the shoulder-to-shoulder crowd almost directly opposite with the swathed shape of the newly-erected Cenotaph between them, fastened his eyes on the bearded uniformed figure.

King, he thought. But didn't he have a body too? Coiled intestines, toe-nails that needed cutting? He had had to go to the lav like anyone else that morning. And he would have eaten his bacon and eggs. But served, of course, from a silver dish. A man, too, had had to serve that man down there, that white body, soft belly, dangling thing inside the stiff uniform breeches. A man had had to bow as he had lifted pink rashers out of a silver dish for him.

He watched the isolated figure in its smooth khaki, with the imprisoning strap of the Sam Browne a dark band across his chest, go stiffly and proudly over to the steps of the Colonial Office where the others were waiting – the Prince of Wales, the Duke of York, Prince Henry, the Archbishop of Canterbury, a figure of floppy white and strait-laced black among the khakis and dark blues of the uniforms, and little stumpy Lloyd George, black again, tail-coat and top hat, with half a dozen other cabinet ministers all looking the same. Dressed up, false, wrong. There had been plenty of time to decide which of them was which since the barriers had been removed at the end of Whitehall just before ten.

And the day would come when they were all puffed away. Their world looked strong enough now. But it would go. They might laugh at the very name *People's Trumpet* now. They might never even have seen a copy, in their palaces, their clubs, their Ministries. But one day a trumpet would sound, and that would be more than just the name of a thin newspaper selling not much more than a thousand copies – no, be honest, not selling a thousand copies. It would be a blast of hatred, swelling up from the people, that would sweep them away, all the pretences and inequalities and cant. All away.

Suddenly the thought, the tiny possibility, that the blast would begin to blow today, that it should begin with him himself in only nineteen minutes' time, at eleven exactly, snickered up to the surface of his mind like the tip of a thin black blade beginning to rip from underneath a smooth stretched white cloth. This might be it. It might be the signal. Coming at that hushed moment of silence, when, as they said, an Empire would be still and pay homage, coming then the words he was going to call out, the words he was going to shout aloud, might do it. They might run like a fissure along the whole sugar-icing façade of the great sham and split it apart for ever.

Down in front of the tapering square block of the new Cenotaph, wholly draped in its bunting, a man in the uniform of a police superintendent walked quickly over to the short dark wooden pillar on which the King was to press the button that would make those too-bright flags fall. He held a brief conference there with a young official in top hat and long black overcoat. After a minute or so they both walked away together into the Home Office.

Maurice's heart raced suddenly. Could information about their plan have somehow got out? Was that short conference down there to discuss how to get him quietly arrested before the Silence began? But at once he told himself that this was impossible. So few of them were in the secret. Only the inner group of the party and the two who had been asked to make the demonstrations, himself and Frances, himself here and Frances in Fleet Street at the *People's Trumpet* office.

The suddenness of his onset of panic worried him. He had thought his nerve had been steadier. He had prided himself, for all his lack of years, on being the equal in courage to the men who had been in the trenches and, boastful or quiet, were so besottedly pleased with themselves for having undergone that experience. And yet a flush of sweat had risen up between his legs and on either side of his chest at the mere thought of arrest.

When the time came would he even be able to break in on that hush of quiet? But he must. He would.

He turned to look north over the heads of the dense and curiously subdued crowd towards Trafalgar Square, hidden in the misty haze, despite the extraordinarily blue sky and clear golden sunshine that graced, as they were saying everywhere, this November day. At any moment – Yes, here it was. Clearly over the uncanny noiselessness of the immense crowd the sound of a high-barked order came. And then the little tinny rattle of a piece of military drill being perfectly executed. What they called 'reversing arms'. There had been, of course, endless reverent explanations in the papers of everything that was to be done. They had proved useful enough in making the plans, but what sickening boot-licking they were to the whole great stage-managed structure. And now the band music was just audible, the faint faraway notes of the Chopin funeral march played crassly on great brass tubas and trumpets.

All round him that distant miniature music was having an almost tangible effect. A woman in close-fitting black two paces in front of him had given one gulping, hastily stifled sob that had sounded extraordinarily loud in the quiet. He could not blame her: for all their brassiness those faraway notes were moving.

Coming nearer bit by bit now were the sounds of the troops who were lining the procession route reversing arms company by company, first the piping cry of the order and then the tiny distant crash of rifles being slapped and thumped. The ritual: that would go. All the pomp. It would go one day, and perhaps the start of its going would come – he slipped a hand under his coat and pulled out his watch – in sixteen, no in fifteen, minutes from now.

The sound of Big Ben chiming the three-quarter hour boomed hollowly out in the clear air, echoing over the slowly rising band music. The King moved forward like a clockwork doll – there would be no soldier toys in the new world – from his place in front of the Colonial Office to a new position facing the uprearing bulk of the hidden Cenotaph and the huge, garish and brutal Union Jack draping its whole front. And after the King came his sons and what they called his Ministers. His. Elected by the people, or some of the people, and yet called his.

And now it had come into sight, what the King and all of them were waiting to receive, the funeral procession of the Unknown Warrior. Poor hopeless victim of cruel and greedy forces he would never have known anything of. But there it was, the procession. First, four policemen on white horses – symbolic figures, little though the onlookers realised it – then the bands, four of them, the regiments of the Foot Guards, their scarlet shining with soft deepness in this mellow-clear light, and next the pipers of the Scots Guards. That keening music had taken over now. And then – Maurice involuntarily caught his breath – the drums. Their muffled insistent beat seemed to enter on the scene all at once as if they had stepped through an invisible sound-proof curtain. At the same instant, it seemed, it was possible to pick out the drummers from the dark haze-swallowed serpent of the procession, the drummers and their black-draped drums and just behind them the bright flag spread over the coffin on its gun-carriage.

He watched, held in fascination, as they approached. The minutes ticked by. The long column of Servicemen split to left and right and took up places lining three-deep the wide roadway on either side of the Cenotaph. And at last the solemn beat of marching feet – that brutal, steel-tipped sound would have no place in the new world – was stilled and the gun-carriage with its Union Jack draped coffin and the steel helmet on it was at rest in front of the massive veiled memorial. Then the bands broke all together into the tune 'O God, our help in ages past'. And the close-packed surpliced choirs on either side of the Home Office steps sang. God, the biggest sham of all, Maurice thought with harsh-grinding force. The great unseen prop. That would come tumbling down too. And the first tiny ripple of energy that must in the end topple the whole piled-on false structure might be his own voice in five – in four minutes from now.

But why did that damned tune have to remind him of so much in the past? Of all the things that had once seemed rock-solid?

The hymn, with the steady rolling of the draped drums underpinning its deep-throated music, came at last to an end. There was a brief silence. Maurice estimated the effect his voice would have breaking the longer, more deliberate silence soon to come. 'It's a sham. It's all a sham. You've been tricked. All of you.' He could almost hear his words ripping into the calm sun-mellowed air. But down by the tall draped block the Archbishop had taken half a pace forward and now it was his voice that was breaking the hush, with the words of the Lord's Prayer. All round people were taking up the sentences, a dull heavy murmur. Words rising up like the chimney smoke today, straight into the still air. And disappearing into nothingness as completely.

Another silence now. The tension as the whole vast throng waited for the coming of the chosen hour – it would be his hour, too – was like a vibration too low to hear but impossible not to be aware of.

And then it came. The rising chime of Big Ben about to strike eleven. Impinging on the rounded gentle notes there was added the sound of distant shouted commands from the direction of Westminster. Then the first thunderous stroke of the hour. The King stiffly extended a hand and touched the button on the dark wooden stand in front of him. On the monument the great areas of bright bunting slowly fell away. Everywhere, from the moment that the huge block of white stone was revealed, heads were bowed. The Silence had begun.

Maurice stood staring at the unveiled block, the crumpled bunting swathing its foot. Every detail of the scene, and all the invisible panoply behind, seemed to enter his whole body and his whole being. The still, sun-glowed air, the silent bowed spectators, the small figure of the King, the symbolic shape of the flag-draped coffin on the gun-carriage and that little khaki-coloured rounded helmet – each piece of the complex so exactly in its place, all at a meeting-point of held suspense. Immovable, unbreakable.

And then with a suddenness that made him start as if an ear-splitting shriek had rent out right at his back the first high, clear notes of the bugles sounding the Last Post penetrated the huge fixed bubble of silence.

It was over. It was too late. His time had gone by. Had he lacked at the pinch courage? It must have been so. It could have been nothing else.

He ceased to see what was around him. He ceased to know what was going on. Like a fog-tasting black scarf the sense of what he had failed to do blotted out everything.

Eventually the crowd beside him must have moved, and he must have been carried along with it. But where he was taken he did not know. What else was happening on this day of solemn remembrance made no impact on him at all. He walked, because at some moment a jostle from the crowd had given him an impetus and there was nothing to stop him.

It was some time in the afternoon – he lacked the initiative even to pull his watch from his waistcoat pocket – that his self-laceration began to take a new form. Perhaps, without realising it, he was starting to emerge from his waking coma and had gained enough awareness to take note of a pair of lovers. But, for whatever reason it was, he abruptly thought of Frances.

He had lost her for ever. That was certain. Work at the *People's Trumpet* had brought them together. Their shared ideals had been their love. And now he had forfeited it all. By his inexplicable cowardice he had lost any right to know her, much less to love her. While she, doing in Fleet Street what he had not been able to do at the Cenotaph, had removed herself as far upwards as he had sunk low.

At this point in his blind progress it occurred to him to buy a copy of *The Star*. Quite what he had expected to see in it he never formulated in his own mind. Perhaps he hoped, and yet feared, to read wide-ranging reports of social revolution springing from the shattering of the almighty mutedness by one fearless girl.

What he did read eventually was a short news-story of brutal simplicity. 'Silence Broken by Girls' it was headed. Four short paragraphs followed, describing in the words of a couple of witnesses the small scene in which the girls of the *People's Trumpet* staff had banged tin lids, danced on a table in view of the street and sung. And then the last paragraph: *Those standing silent in Fleet Street waited until the end of the ceremony. Then they burst into the office. The men stood aside while indignant girls and women gave the disturbers of the peace a thorough beating, which ceased only when the police arrived.*

There was no more to it that that. Maurice dropped the paper, took one wild glance around him till he recognised where he was and set off, fast as his striding legs would go, for Fleet Street.

When, some twenty minutes later, he arrived at the *People's Trumpet* office, that narrow garishly red-painted small shop, he found the outer door locked. He knocked and there was no answer. But he could think of nothing else to do but knock again. And this time the door was cautiously opened a crack and he saw Frances's white face, grubby with dried tears and with a long blood-scabbed scratch down one cheek. She let him in.

'Maurice, you look all right. Did they set on you, or what?'

For an instant he was tempted to evade the truth. But he knew that with Frances there was no possibility of that.

'I didn't – I couldn't – Oh, God, Frances, I never uttered a sound.'

Standing there with her back against the hastily closed shop door, she took him in her arms. And he allowed himself for a tiny space of time to feel the comfort of it. But then he broke away.

'No,' he said. 'It's all over between us. It must be.'

But again she held out her arms to him.

'Maurice, it's no shame that you couldn't do it when the

time came. We each of us do what we can. The others'll understand.'

Her voice tailed away as her never-baulking mind told her how unlikely it was that the others would understand. But she went bravely on.

'Well, I understand. That was something I could do, though God knows if I could again. Now.'

Then the tears that had dried on her face broke out once more, and it was his turn to hold out his arms and offer comfort and to try and blot out, impossible though it was with mere murmured words, the memory of what had been done to her.

But as he stroked the hard, jerking surface of her rounded shoulders and as he produced the meaningless, designed-to-ease babble, he realised that it was from his hands that one last blow was to have to fall on her. And when after a long while her tears had slackened he said, as quickly as he could to get it over with, the thing that he found he had to say.

He led her to a bentwood chair and made her sit down. Then he stood a little way away from her.

'Frances,' he choked out, 'it wasn't because I was afraid. I thought it was, afterwards. I still thought it was when I got here. But seeing you and talking to you I realise what the truth of it is. It wasn't because I didn't have the guts to do it: it was because it was all so right there. Frances, it was right. Everything. The sunlight, the people standing so still, the Cenotaph, the flags on it. Even the King. It was all so right, Frances.'

For a few seconds he was silent, and so was she, sitting on the dark chair with her head dropped forward and her hands clutching the varnished rim of the seat. Then he spoke again.

'So it's goodbye, isn't it?' he said.

'Yes,' she whispered. 'It's goodbye.'

He went out of the office and walked, with tears streaming down his face, along Fleet Street. Above him, from the walls of the tall newspaper offices bunting hung, garishly bright in the gathering gloom of the November twilight.

OLD FLAME

William Trevor

Grace died.

As Zoë replaces the lid of the electric kettle – having steamed the envelope open – her eye is caught by that stark statement. As she unfolds the plain white writing-paper, another random remark registers before she begins to read from the beginning. *We never quarrelled not once that I remember.*

The spidery scrawl, that economy with punctuation, were once drooled over by her husband, and to this day are not received in any ordinary manner, as a newspaper bill is, or a rates demand. Because of the sexual passion there has been, the scrawl connects with Charles's own neat script, two parts of a conjunction in which letters have played an emotional part. Being given to promptness in such matters, Charles will at once compose a reply, considerate of an old flame's due. Zoë feared this correspondence once, and hated it. *As ever my love, Audrey*: in all the years of the relationship the final words have been the same.

As always, she'll have to reseal the envelope because the adhesive on the flap has lost its efficacy. Much easier all that is nowadays, with convenient sticks of Pritt or Uhu. Once, at the height of the affair, she'd got glue all over the letter itself.

Zoë, now seventy-one, is a small, slender woman, only a little bent. Her straight hair, once jet-black, is almost white. What she herself thinks of as a letter-box mouth caused her, earlier in her life, to be designated attractive rather than beautiful. 'Wild,' she was called as a girl, and 'unpredictable', both terms relating to her temperament. No one has ever called her pretty, and no one would call her wild or unpredictable now.

Because it's early in the day she is still in her dressing-gown, a pattern of dragons in blue and scarlet silk. It hugs her slight body, crossed over on itself in front, tied with a matching sash. When her husband appears he'll still be in his dressing-gown also, comfortably woollen, teddy-bear brown stitched with braid. *Dearest, dearest Charles* the letter begins. Zoë reads all of it again.

This letter is special, of course, because of Grace's death. Others have been different. *Grace and I wondered how you are getting along these days . . . Grace and I have finally taken retirement . . . I'm to give you this address Grace says. Just in case you ever want to write . . . A sea-side house. Grace always wanted that . . .* In 1985, in 1978 and '73 and '69, Grace always had a kind of say. *A quick lunch some time?* each letter – this one too – suggests before the *As ever my love* and the single cross that's a reminder of their kissing. Somehow, Zoë has always believed, the quick-lunch suggestion came from Grace. Did she, she wonders, make it again on her deathbed?

The affair has developed in Zoë an extra sense. Without making an effort she can visualise a tall woman she has never met, now the lone occupant of a house she has never entered. She sees her smartly dressed in shades of maroon, iron-grey hair fashionably arranged, the clarity of her eyes a little clouded. Creases have multiplied on the skin of her face and are a map of wrinkles now. Zoë imagines her entering her kitchen and turning on the radio, to hear the same news she herself heard earlier: football fans on the rampage in a German city, shop windows smashed, a bus turned on its side. She imagines her standing with a cup of Nescafé in the bow-window of her sitting-room: seen through drizzle on a pane, the sea's a pattern of undulations, greyish green, scuffed with white. The sky that meets it on the far horizon is too dull to contemplate. A single mackerel-trawler slips into view.

If it's inconvenient or if you'd rather not well of course I understand.

The Alp Horn is where they lunch, have done so since 1951. Her inquisitiveness getting the better of her, Zoë went there once. She actually went inside, giving a name she had made up, of someone she was to meet there. A musical instrument, presumably an alp-horn, stretched the length of a wall; Tyrolean landscape decorated two others. There were checked tablecloths, blue and red; recorded music played; the place was modest. 'I'm awfully sorry,' Zoë said to a waiter, half a lifetime ago it seems like because in fact it is. 'Clearly there's been a muddle.'

She finds the Pritt where Charles keeps it, in the middle drawer of the dresser, with his writing things and sealing-wax, Sellotape and scissors. She boils the water in the kettle again, for coffee. She hears his footstep above her, crossing the landing from their bedroom to the lavatory, crossing it again to the bathroom. Pipes rattle when he turns on the hot water because he has never learnt not to turn the tap all the way in order to prevent its gushing so. All the years she has known him he has been impatient about things like that.

'It's time you saw Charles again,' Zoë knows Grace used to say in that house, and guesses Audrey's reply: that Charles has his own life now, that Charles made his choice. Grace always pressed, gently, because she loved Charles, too, but had to keep it to herself. 'My dear, I'm certain Charles would welcome a sign.' Anything could have happened: they'd never know.

Forty years have passed since the year of the great passion: 1951. Charles and Audrey and Grace had met in that colourless time of disaffected lives and utility clothes when nobody was having much fun except the remaining spivs. Audrey and Grace had been in the ATS during the war, together all the time. When Charles arrived on the scene they were back in office life, both of them determined to use their secretarial posts as stepping-stones to something better. The day Charles appeared – the first time they laid eyes on him – he was being led around by the snooty, half-drunk Miss Maybury, both of them with glasses of vin rosé, which was what La Maybury – her office title – drank every afternoon, sometimes in the mornings also. 'Hullo,' Charles said, a lanky young man with floppy fair hair. It wasn't difficult for Zoë to imagine the shy smile he'd darted at Audrey and then at Grace. Afterwards he'd told her about La Maybury and the wine and the tour round the office.

'Poor Charles' he had become in after years. Poor Charles alone with his unloved, unloving wife. What was the point of any of it, now that his children were grown up? In their seaside house they lived in hope – that one day he would sound less whispery on the telephone, passing on details of death by misadventure or disease. 'Given six months, a merciful release.' Or: 'Just slipped. A wretched plastic bag. In the rain, near the dustbins.'

Zoë places two slices of bread in the toaster but does not press the lever down because it isn't time to yet. Before the affair got going it had been a subject of fascination to him that two such apparently close friends should, in appearance at least, be so vastly different. 'Oh, that's often so,' Zoë said, citing examples from her schooldays, but he had never shown much interest in her schooldays and he didn't then. 'Grace, the lumpy one's called,' he said. 'Back of a bus. Audrey's the stunner.' Old-fashioned names, she had thought, and imagined old-fashioned girls, frumpish in spite of Audrey's looks. Later, he'd always included Grace in his references to Audrey, clouding the surface because of the depths beneath.

She measures coffee into a blue Denby pot, the last piece of a set. There was a photograph she found once, Audrey as handsome as he'd claimed, a goddess-like creature with a cigarette, Grace blurred, as if she'd moved. They were sprawled on a rug beside a tablecloth from which a picnic had been eaten. You could see part of the back wheel of a car and it wasn't difficult to sharpen into focus Grace's frizzy hair, two pink-rimmed eyes behind her spectacles. Where on earth had that picnic been? What opportunity had been seized – a slack afternoon in the office?

Zoë props the letter against his cup, doing so with deliberation. It will vex him that she has arranged it so, the gesture attaching a comment of her own; but then she has been vexed herself. She tore that photograph into little pieces and watched them burn. He never mentioned its loss, as naturally he wouldn't.

'Ah, good,' she greets him, and watches while he picks the letter up. She depresses the lever of the toaster. The milk saucepan rattles on the gas, a glass disc bouncing about in it to prevent the milk from boiling over. She pours their coffee. He returns the letter to its envelope. She halves each piece of toast diagonally, the way he likes it.

She hadn't guessed. It was a frightening, numbing shock when he said: 'Look, I have to tell you. Audrey and I have fallen in love.' Just for a moment she couldn't think who Audrey was. 'Audrey and I,' he repeated, thinking she hadn't properly heard. 'Audrey and I love one another.' For what remained of that year and for several years following it, Zoë felt physically sick every time that statement echoed, coming back to her from its own Sunday morning: September 9th, 1951, eleven o'clock. He had chosen the time because they'd have all day to go into things, yet apart from practicalities there was nothing to go into. You couldn't much go into the fact that he wanted someone else more than he wanted her. After five years of marriage he was tired of her. He had spoken in order to be rid of her.

Finishing with the marmalade, she moves it closer to him. His face, less expert at disguise than once it was, hides nothing. She watches him thinking about the woman who has been left on her own, his sympathy reaching into a seaside house that's now too spacious for one. But Charles is not an imaginative man. He doesn't penetrate far. He doesn't see in the old flame's fridge a chicken joint for one, and fish for one tomorrow. Winter's a melancholy time to be bereaved, a mood reflected in the cold and wet, winds rattling and whining. Audrey'll miss her friend particularly when it comes to watching television, no one beside her to share a comment with.

'Oh yes, the Alp Horn's still there,' Zoë hears a little later that morning, having eased open a door he has carefully closed. 'Twelve forty-five, should we say? If your train's a little late, anything like that, please don't worry. I'll simply wait, my dear.'

He'd been saying something she hadn't managed to hear before that, his voice unnaturally low, a hand cupped round the mouthpiece. Then there'd been the hint of a reprimand because the old flame hadn't written sooner. Had he known he'd have gone to the funeral.

'I'm sorry to have hurt you so,' he said later that Sunday, but words by then made no sense whatsoever. Five years of a mistake, she thought, two children mistakenly born. Her tears dripped on to her clothes while he stood there crestfallen, his good looks distorted by distress. She did not blow her nose; she wanted to look as she felt. 'You would like me dead,' she sobbed, willing him to raise his fist in fury at her, to crash it down on her, obliterating in mercy all that remained of her. But he only stood there, seeming suddenly ill-fed. Had she not cooked properly for him? Her thoughts half-crazily ran on. Had she not given him what was nourishing? 'I thought we were happy,' she whispered. 'I thought we didn't need to question anything.'

'Nice to see the old Alp Horn again,' his murmur comes from the hall, and Zoë can tell that he's endeavouring to be cheerful. 'Tell you what, I'll bring a packet of Three Castles.'

There is the click of the receiver, the brief sounding of the bell. He says something to himself, something like 'Poor thing!' Zoë softly closes the door. Grace and Audrey had probably been friends for fifty years, might even have been schoolfriends. Was Audrey the one whom other girls had pashes on? Was Grace a little bullied? Zoë imagines her hunched sulkily into a desk, and Audrey standing up for her. In letters and telephone conversations there have been references to friends, to holidays in Normandy and Brittany, to bridge, to Grace's colonic irrigation, to Audrey's wisdom teeth removed in hospital. Zoë knows – she doesn't often call it guessing – that after Audrey's return from every visit to the Alp Horn Grace was greedy for the morsels passed on to her. Not by the blink of an eye could Grace reveal her secret; the only expression of her passion was her constancy in urging another letter. *We think of you with her in that coldness.* 'Quite frail he looked,' Audrey no doubt reported in recent years.

He did not stay with Zoë in 1951 because of love. He stayed because – quite suddenly, and unexpectedly – the emotions all around him seemed to have become too much: it was weariness that caused him to back off. Had he sensed, Zoë wondered years later, the shadow of Grace without entirely knowing that that was what it was? He stayed, he said, because Zoë and the two children who had then been born meant more than he had estimated. Beneath this statement there was the implication that for the sake of his own happiness it wasn't fair to impose hardship on the innocent. That, though unspoken, had a bitter ring for Zoë. 'Oh, go away!' she cried. 'Go to that unpleasant woman.' But she did not insist, she did not say there was nothing left, that the damage had been done for ever. To the woman, he quoted his economic circumstances as the reason for thinking again. Supporting two households – which in those days was what the prospect looked like – was more than daunting. *Grace says you wouldn't have to leave your children penniless. What she and I earn could easily make up for that. Grace would love to help us out.* Had he gone, Grace would somehow have been there too.

Zoë knows when the day arrives. Glancing across their breakfast coffee at her, his eyes have a dull sparkle that's caused by an attempt to rekindle an obsolete excitement: he was always one to make an effort. In a letter once Audrey referred to his 'loose-limbed charm', stating that she doubted she could live without it and be herself. He still has that lanky look, which perhaps was what she meant; what remains of his floppy fair hair, mainly at the back and sides of his head, is ash-coloured now; his hands – which Zoë can well imagine either Grace or Audrey designating his most elegant feature – have a shrivelled look, the bones more pronounced than once they were, splotches of freckles on skin like old paper. His face is beakier than it was, the teeth for the most part false, his eyes given to watering when a room is warm. Two spots of pink come and go high up on his narrow cheeks, where the structure of the cheekbones tautens the skin. Otherwise, his face is pale.

'I have to go in today,' he casually announces.

'Not here for lunch?'

'I'll pick up a sandwich somewhere.'

She would like to be able to suggest he'd be wiser to go to a more expensive restaurant than the Alp Horn. Cheap food and house wine are a deadly combination at his time of life. A dreadful nuisance it is when his stomach goes wrong.

'Bit of shopping to do,' he says.

Once there was old so-and-so to meet but that doesn't work any more because, with age, such figures can't be counted upon not to give the game away. There was 'the man at Lloyd's' to see, or Hanson and Phillips, who were arranging an annuity. All that has been tapped too often: what's left is the feebleness of shopping. Before his retirement there was no need to mention anything at all.

'Shopping,' she says without an interrogative note. 'Shopping.'

'One or two things.'

Three Castles cigarettes are difficult to find. Audrey will smoke nothing else and it's half a joke that he goes in search of them, a fragment of affection in the kaleidoscope of the love affair. Another such fragment is their shared delight in sweetbreads, a food Zoë finds repellent. They share unpunctuality also. *Grace can't understand how we ever manage to meet!*

'Should keep fine,' he predicts.

'Take your umbrella all the same.'

'Yes, I'll take my umbrella.'

He asks about a particular shirt, his blue striped one. He wonders if it has been ironed. She tells him where it is. Their three children – the boys, and Cecilia, born later, all married now – know nothing about Audrey. Sometimes it seems odd to Zoë that this should be so, that a person who has featured so profoundly in their father's life, should be unknown to them. If that person had had her way Cecilia would not have been born at all.

'Anything you need?' he offers. 'Anything I can get you?'

She shakes her head. She wishes she could say: 'I open her letters. I listen when there's a phone conversation.'

She wishes he could tell her that Grace has died, that his friend is now alone.

'Back about four, I expect?'

'Something like that.'

Had he gone off, she wouldn't still be in this house. She wouldn't be sitting in this kitchen in her scarlet-dragon dressing-gown, eying him in his woolly brown one. She'd be living with one of the children or in a flat somewhere. Years ago the house would have been sold; she'd not have grown old with a companion. It was most unlikely there would ever have been another man; she doubted she'd have wanted one.

'I dreamed we were on a ferry going to Denmark,' he unexpectedly says. 'There was a woman you got talking to, all in brown.'

'Prettily in brown?'

'Oh, yes. A pretty woman, too. She used an odd expression. She said she was determined to have what she called a "corking child".'

'Ah.'

'You sat me down in front of her and made me comment on her dress. You made me make suggestions.'

'And did you, Charles?'

'I did. I suggested shades of green. Deep greens; not olive like my trousers. And rounded collar-ends on her shirt, not pointed like mine. I made her look at mine. She was a nice woman except that she said something a little rude about my shoes.'

'Scuffed?'

'Something like that.'

'Your shoes are never scuffed.'

'No.'

'Well, there you are.'

He nods. 'Yes, there you are.'

Soon after that he rises and goes upstairs again. Why did that conversation about a dream take place? It's true that just occasionally they tell one another their dreams; just occasionally, they have always done so. But significance appears to attach to the fact that he shared his with her this morning: that is a feeling she has.

'Why did you bother with me if I didn't matter?' Long

after he'd decided to stay with her she asked him that. Long afterwards she questioned everything; she tore at the love that had united them in the first place; it was her right that he should listen to her. Five years went by before their daughter was born.

'Well, I'm off.'

Like a tall, thin child he looks, his eyes deep in their sockets, his dark, conventional suit well-pressed, a paisley tie in swirls of blue that matches the striped blue shirt. His brown shoes, the pair he keeps for special occasions, gleam as they did not in his eccentric dream.

'If I'd known I'd have come with you.' Zoë can't help saying that; she doesn't intend to, the words come out. But they don't alarm him, as once they would have. Once, a shadow of terror would have passed through his features, apprehension spreading lest she rush upstairs to put her coat on.

'We'll go in together next time,' he promises.

'Yes, that'll be nice.'

They kiss, as they always do when they part. The hall door bangs behind him. She'll open a tin of salmon for lunch and have it with tomatoes and a packet of crisps. A whole tin will be too much, of course, but between them they'll probably be able to eat whatever's left this evening.

In the sitting-room she turns the television on. Celeste Holm, lavishly fur-coated, is in a car, cross about something. Zoë doesn't want to watch and turns it off again. She imagines the old flame excited as the train approaches London. An hour ago the old flame made her face up, but now she does it all over again, difficult with the movement of the train. Audrey doesn't know that love came back into the marriage, that skin grew over the wound. She doesn't know, because no one told her, because he cannot bring himself to say that the brief occasion was an aberration. He honours – because he's made like that – whatever it is the affair still means to the woman whose life it has disrupted. He doesn't know that Audrey – in receipt of all that was on offer – would have recovered from the drama in a natural way if Grace – in receipt of nothing at all – hadn't been an influence. He doesn't wonder what will happen now, since death has altered the pattern of loose ends.

Opening the salmon tin, Zoë travels again to the Alp Horn rendezvous. She wonders if it has changed and considers it unlikely. The long horn still stretches over a single wall. The same Tyrolean landscape decorates two others. There are the blue-and-red tablecloths. He waits with a glass of sherry, and then she's there.

'My dear!'

She is the first to issue their familiar greeting, catching him unaware the way things sometimes do these days.

'My dear!' he says in turn.

Sherry is ordered for her too, and when it comes the rims of their glasses touch for a moment, a toast to the past.

'Grace,' he says. 'I'm sorry.'

'Yes.'

'Is it awful?'

'I manage.'

The waiter briskly notes their order and enquires about the wine.

'Oh, the good old house red.'

Zoë's fingers, gripping and slicing a tomato, are arthritic, painful sometimes though not at present. In bed at night he's gentle when he reaches out for one hand or the other, cautious with affection, not tightening his grasp as once he did. Her fingers are ugly; she sometimes thinks she looks quite like a monkey now. She arranges the fish and the tomato on a plate and sprinkles pepper over both. Neither she nor Charles ever has salt.

'And you, Charles?'

'I'm all right.'

'I worry about you sometimes.'

'No, I'm all right.'

It was accordian music that was playing in the Alp Horn the day Zoë's inquisitiveness drove her into it. Young office people occupied the tables. Business was quite brisk.

'I do appreciate this,' Audrey says. 'When something's over, all these years – I do appreciate it, Charles.'

He passes across the table the packet of Three Castles

cigarettes, and she smiles, placing it beside her because it's too soon yet to open it.

'You're fun, Charles.'

'I think La Maybury married, you know. I think someone told me that.'

'Grace could never stand her.'

'No.'

Is this the end? Zoë wonders. Is this the final fling, the final call on his integrity and honour? Can his guilt slip back into whatever recesses there are, safe at last from Grace's secondhand desire? No one told him that keeping faith could be as cruel as confessing faithlessness; only Grace might have appropriately done that, falsely playing a best friend's role. But it wasn't in Grace's interest to do so.

'Perhaps I'll sell the house.'

'I rather think you should.'

'Grace did suggest it once.'

Leaving them to it, Zoë eats her salmon and tomato. She watches the end of the television film: years ago they saw it together, before 1951, before Grace and Audrey. They've seen it together since; as a boy he'd been in love with Bette Davis. Picking at the food she has prepared, Zoë is again amused by what has amused her before. But only part of her attention is absorbed. Conversations take place; she does not hear; what she sees are fingers undistorted by arthritis loosening the cellophane on the cigarette packet and twisting it into a butterfly. He orders coffee. The scent that came back on his clothes was lemony with a trace of lilac. In a letter there was a mention of the cellophane twisted into a butterfly.

'Well, there we are,' he says. 'It's been lovely to see you, Audrey.'

'Lovely for me too.'

When he has paid the bill they sit for just a moment longer. Then, in the Ladies, she powders away the shine that heat and wine have induced, and tidies her tidy grey hair. The lemony scent refreshes, for a moment, the stale air of the cloakroom.

'Well, there we are, my dear,' he says again on the street. Has there ever, Zoë wonders, been snappishness between them? Is she the kind not to lose her temper, long-suffering and patient as well as being a favourite girl at school? After all, she never quarrelled with her friend.

'Yes, there we are, Charles.' She takes his arm. 'All this means the world to me, you know.'

They walk to the corner, looking for a taxi. Marriage is full of quarrels, Zoë reflects.

'Being upright never helps. You just lie there. Drink lots of water, Charles.'

The jug of water, filled before she'd slipped in beside him last night, is on his bedside table, one glass poured out. Once, though quite a while ago now, he not only insisted on getting up when he had a stomach upset but actually worked in the garden. All day, she'd watched him filling his incinerator with leaves and weeding the rockery. Several times she'd rapped on the kitchen window, but he'd taken no notice. As a result he was laid up for a fortnight.

'I'm sorry to be a nuisance,' he says.

She smoothes the bedclothes on her side of the bed, giving the bed up to him, making it pleasant for him in the hope that he'll remain in it. The newspaper is there for him when he feels like it. So is *Little Dorrit*, which he always reads when he's unwell.

'Perhaps consommé later on,' she says. 'And a cream cracker.'

'You're very good to me.'

'Oh, now.'

Downstairs Zoë lights the gas-fire in the sitting-room and looks to see if there's a morning film. *Barefoot in the Park* it is, about to begin. Quite suddenly then, without warning, she sees how the loose ends are. Everything is different, but nothing of course will ever be said. *So good the little restaurant's still there*, the old flame writes. *Just a line to thank you*. So good it was to talk. So good to see him. So good of him to remember the Three Castles. Yet none of it is any good at all because Grace is not there to say, 'Now tell me every single thing.' Not there to say when there's a nagging doubt, 'My dear, what perfect nonsense!' On her own in the seaside house she'll not find an excuse again to suggest a quick lunch if he'd like to. He'll not do so himself, since he never has. He'll gladly feel his duty done at last.

The old flame bores him now, with her scent and her cigarettes and her cellophane butterflies. In her seaside house she knows her thank-you letter is the last, and the sea is grey and again it rains. One day, on her own, she'll guess her friend was false. One day she'll guess a sense of honour kept pretence alive.

Grace died. That's all that happened, Zoë tells herself, so why should she forgive? 'Why should I?' she murmurs. 'Why should I?' Yet for a moment before she turns on *Barefoot in the Park* tears sting her eyelids. A trick of old age, she tells herself, and orders them away.

THE VILLAGE

A Christmas Story

George Mackay Brown

At five o'clock on Christmas morning a light went on in the top window of a tall house. Peedie Sigurd and his sister Gerd were the first folk to awake in the village. They were tearing string and paper from the gifts Santa had left. Sigurd had hardly slept all night. At ten to five he had shaken his sister awake. Between sleep and enchantment they sat on their beds, with apples, boxes of sweeties, books, a draughts-board, a doll, diaries, nuts, and a growing litter of string and fancy paper. Sigurd opened a soft parcel and pulled out a new knitted balaclava. He cried out in rage and threw it on the floor. (Sigurd hated above all things to be given clothes for a present.) Gerd fell back asleep on her pillow, clutching the doll.

In the three fishermen's houses above the pier, dark windows at six o'clock still. Normally, on such a quiet morning, there would have been moving shadows between lamps and uncurtained windows. But this was Christmas morning, when even fishermen could lie long. And their wives dreamed of seapinks. And their children dreamed of castles made of chocolate and marzipan, where the tables are loaded with all the good things in the world, swans and apples, everything except fish.

At nine o'clock there was a hideous rattling and clangour and metal outcry just beside poor Miss Papay's head. Miss

Papay's nervous system was in ruins each morning because of that alarm clock. 'It's a wonder,' she said to Sam her white cat, 'I'm not in the nut-house, with that alarm clock!' . . . Then Miss Papay remembered that it was Christmas morning. 'A merry Christmas, Sam,' she said. 'I have a little something for you, Sam.' Miss Papay went to the kitchen cupboard in her dressing-gown and brought out a little fish on a plate. It was a herring. The scales shone like stars. Miss Papay set the herring-plate on the stone floor beside the sink. 'A merry Christmas to you,' said Sam the cat. Or maybe he said, 'Oh good, I like herring.' Or maybe he said, 'Here's just another day and another breakfast.' At any rate Sam meowed beautifully. And Miss Papay lit the fire with a tranquil hand and put on the kettle for her breakfast. Miss Papay's nerves soon recovered from the berserk yells of the alarm clock; she being a gentle old lady, in love with the cluster of flames in her fire and her singing kettle and knowledge that she had lived to see another Christmas, in spite of an ancient heartbreak.

At ten o'clock Tom Keldie opened the village shop that sold everything: fishermen's jerseys, and a hundred kind of sweeties, and potatoes and newspapers and bottles of whisky and beer and sugar and lentils and tea. Tom Keldie gave a baleful glance at a rack containing 45 unsold Christmas cards. Tom Keldie's shop was also the Post Office. Today there was only one letter to date-stamp, addressed to the Member of Parliament. What could Mrs Wilson of Fetters farm be wanting to write to the MP about? The MP wasn't in London, he was home in Orkney for Christmas – only a very stupid person such as Tibby Wilson wouldn't have realised that. Mrs Tibby Wilson was always writing letters to people in high places, but nothing seemed to come of any of her letters. Tom Keldie must have date-stamped and sorted a hundred of her letters to dukes and bishops and film stars in the course of the past year.

Tom Keldie dipped a steel pen in a bottle of ink. He stroked out 'Christmas' on 45 cards, and wrote 'New Year' instead. A Merry New Year. A few folk for sure would have forgotten to send this one or that one at Christmas card; well, now they had a chance to make reparation.

Willie Swart the beachcomber came in and bought a bottle of whisky for twelve shillings and sixpence.

That was all the business that Tom Keldie did that day.

At eleven o'clock Jock Arnison the beadle began to ring the kirk bell. Many a task Jock Arnison had to do, such as digging graves and bearing the big bible up to the pulpit, walking doucely in front of the minister. And going round the village with the communion cards. And giving boys the sharp edge of his tongue for playing 'cops and robbers' among the tombstones. And brushing stour and cobwebs and sweetie papers on a Monday morning from the aisles of the gallery.

But this was the job Jock Arnison liked best of all, to ring the bell on Sunday morning. He pulled the rope; gravely the bronze head above nodded, and the clapper gave out such sweet pure brimming sounds that it was a joy to hear; it must (thought Jock) be the next best thing to the singing of the angels in heaven. How the village and the hill and the lock and the peat-bog and the Sound beyond had glory put upon them, Sabbath after Sabbath, by that roundel from the kirk steeple!

And this was Christmas morning, and the bell rang with more joy than any other morning.

In ones and twos, the villagers began to move towards the open door of the church, bonneted and bibled and bell-blessed.

The minister walked down the steep brae from the manse nodding to this one and that on the road. 'Well, well,' said the minister to the horse at the Mill, that had helped to bring home the golden sheaves in August.

At twelve o'clock noon, suddenly, the village was possessed by children. Each boy and girl was burdened with Christmas gifts. They showed books and dolls and games to each other. 'I'll tell you this,' said a boy called Sander Sweyn, 'promise you won't tell the old ones, because then we mightn't get presents another Christmas. This is a secret, I know because I saw it happening . . .'

The scattered children clustered about Sander Sweyn, who always had dangerous and exciting news to tell.

'Listen,' said Sander in a swart whisper, 'there's no such person as Santa, it's your father and mother that put things in your stockings at Christmas, all that about Santa's a fairy-tale . . .'

There was an appalled silence all around Sander Sweyn for – it might be – five seconds. Then, 'You're a liar!' yelled Sigurd. 'I was awake all night and I know, I heard him in our room. I didn't see him because I kept my eyes shut. If you see him you get cinders in your stocking. But I heard him all right.'

Gerd hit Sander Sweyn with her rag doll, again and again. Then the rag doll fell on the road, and Gerd began to cry.

Other boys began to hit Sander Sweyn, and one kicked him hard on the shin.

It's hard to know what would have come of the iconoclast if Mr Allister the teacher hadn't rapped sharply on his study window from the festive glow inside. He gathered his brows against them. His mouth went into different shapes. The children couldn't hear what he was saying but they knew it must be something angry.

They scattered like a shower of starlings, all but Gerd who stood over her rag doll, crying.

At one o'clock in the afternoon, what loaded tables, what merriment, what bright faces, what feasting! Ham broth they had in the twenty-five village houses (with slight variations), roast beef and roast tatties and turnip and cabbage, plum pudding with threepenny-bits and rings and trinkets hidden among the seething spice and nuts and sultanas. Ginger wine for the children, bottles of stout for the men, tea for the women. And such great leaping fires that there was hardly need for the lamps on the sideboard.

In one house, however, there was no such thing.

Willie Swart sat beside the seawood fire and tilted his whisky bottle from time to time, between broken bits of song and insult.

At two o'clock sleep went over the village in a sunset wave: all but the children who played ludo or snakes-and-ladders, and grew slowly nauseated with chocolate and ginger wine, and sometimes they growled at each other like dogs with bones. (The truth is, there had been too much excitement in too short a time, it was more than small creatures could endure.)

Even Willie Swart slept a smouldering sleep in his rocking-chair beside the half-empty whisky bottle.

And Miss Papay slept, dreaming of the time long ago when she had been a school-teacher in Edinburgh, and had a lover that had gone away and left her: or been drowned in the Pacific Ocean, he being a sailor.

Sam her cat curled the last drop of milk round his tongue, and curled his lithe beautiful shape round his small pulsing heart beside the fire, asleep too.

At three o'clock the first snowflake of winter fell on the blacksmith's cold window, and clung there. A score, a hundred cold grey lingerers and loiterers followed; then a thousand came dancing down the hushed air, ten thousand, a million! It was as if an immaculate white cloth had been spread over the fields and the roofs and the village street. Then the snow-cloud moved over towards Hamnavoe and Hoy and Suleskerry. How brightly the lamps shone then in the village houses. (All except Willie Swart's – his lamp was his whisky bottle.)

At four o'clock the first star shone over the hill.

Between the star outside and the leaping and purring fire inside his study, the Rev. Aeneas McTweedie fell asleep after his dinner and his glass of port. He dreamed he saw the three Magi, but they were three ragged tramps. As they came down from the hill to the village, the miller's horse came to meet them, and it was a skeleton – the rattling skeleton of a horse! And one of the tramps put a buttercup in the bone jaws; one gave the horse a shell; the third one gave a finger-lick of dew to the rattling framework. And then the horse-skeleton, clothed in wind and flame again, went romping round and round the meadow!

Then the Magi-tramps stood on the steep brae above the village. They said, 'Our names are Faith and Hope and Charity – we can't stay here long – we have to visit every place in the world. There's much need. We hope we're not too late. But we bless this village, too.'

Five o'clock till eleven o'clock the next morning, the great wave of a midwinter night crashed soundlessly, with surf and spindrift of stars, upon the little community of boats and nets.

Inside, they sat beside their lamps and fires and told stories.

At twelve o'clock Willie Swart threw the empty whisky bottle into the stone corner of his room; it broke like a lamp, with many black smashings and tinklings.

And Willie Swart slept with a flaming face in his rocking-chair, slouched sideways.

And into every villager – Sigurd and Gerd, and the three fishermen, and Miss Papay and Sam the cat, Tom Keldie, Willie Swart, Jock Arnison, Sander Sweyn and the minister and the miller's horse – passed the dreaming shuttle.

SOUND PROOF

Angela Keys

The child was restless.

He had been fed twice that morning. He was always a hungry baby and had sucked strongly from the time that he was born. Her nipples were sore and she knew she would feed him again if he cried. It was the only way she could satisfy him. He was growing fast and strong and her pleasure in him and her love of him grew with the same steady force.

Slowly she lifted him from his cot on the floor and held him in the air above her. His response was immediate, his face bursting with a smile. He was wet. She changed his towelling nappy and dressed him carefully and slowly, talking to him all the while in a soft caressing voice. She always talked quietly to him when he was awake. All his waking hours her voice washed over him: over and over in comforting waves. Never did her voice get harsh or sharp or anxious. It was always flapping against the shores of his consciousness. When he cried he could not hear her, but when he stopped he felt the voice soothe him again. She talked to him about how she felt: about what she had done in her life; about what she would go on to do. She talked about her absent family and friends and who he was like and of things she wanted to be reminded of. Her isolation in this strange part of Britain was not so painful and bitter now. Now that she had him to care for. Her husband usually left early in the morning and came back late at night. Often she and the child were sleeping when he left for work and sleeping when he returned. She had begun to notice how loudly he spoke and how rough and careless he seemed with the child. He would throw him into the air and catch him. He would shake him from side to side, twisting the child in the air. And he would sing those noisy Irish songs and recite Rabbie Burns to him in this isolated Welsh village. The child thrilled to it all.

She placed him in the pram, propped up by a small pillow (she had embroidered the case herself with his name, Patrick.) She tied on the white bonnet. It made him look pale but in the late autumn a slight chill was seeping into the air. She pushed the pram into the path, pushing down hard on the handbar so that she could lower it down the steps on two wheels. There was no need to lock the door, she would not be long. The letter to her mother had to be posted and it was not far to the blood red postbox. As she walked she talked to him in the pram. His feet jiggled the letter lying on his blanket. He watched her carefully, hands held out in the air at either side of his body. He responded to her sounds with sounds of his own, his whole body involved in the interaction. They were complete. They began and ended with one another. They took and gave back to each other, never diminishing, always growing.

She became aware of a noise some way off. She realised at once that it was the sound of a horse galloping very fast. There were other noises with it. Dragging, scraping, urgent noises that she could not identify, but felt a growing panic surging up into her throat. She instinctively stood frozen to the spot leaning into the hedge, her knuckles white on the black, black handle of the pram as she tried to pull it into the hedge with her. The child watching her started to cry, sensing her fear. The horse broke upon them around the bend with such suddenness that she screamed out. Its eyes were white, weird and wild and reflected the fear in her own. It frothed at the mouth, the foamy bubbling, sprayed away from its mouth and caught on the chestnut flanks. It drew the air in through its nostrils with sharp whines. It galloped towards the pair with crazed, blind speed not noticing her at first, standing there crouched in the hedge. When it did see her it veered away and it was then that she saw the trap. It was still harnessed to the horse and swinging from side to side. The trap caught her on one of her legs and threw her on to the road and there she watched helplessly as it gathered up the pram.

She started to run after her child and saw the pram turn over. He was strapped in, she remembered, as she heard the thud. With the pram on its side, wildly thrashing about the road she noticed the blood. And he was not crying.

The horse was getting tired, she could tell it was slowing. Even so, it was far ahead of her still, the trap and pram bouncing oddly on the hard surface. Other voices burst upon her consciousness. A man had run up to the horse with his hands above his head, stopping it. The creature was exhausted and relieved to be under control. The workmen saw her coming and stood silently as she knelt on the road slowly undoing the strap that had held her child. The pram cover and blanket were shredded and muddy. The 'k' in Patrick had been obliterated by blood. One man took off his coat and placed it on the road next to the wrecked pram. She laid the lifeless child on it and looked at him.

She stood up and looked down at him. She knew he was dead.

She suddenly gathered him up holding him tightly to her body. She felt her milk come with a sharp, stinging hardness as she pressed him to her. She held him so that his mouth was near her nipple, her painful stinging breast that was leaking his milk. A damp patch grew on her dark blouse.

They asked her name, where she was from. Women arrived in aprons smelling of bread and soap and told her that the doctor had been sent for. Her distress repelled them, no one moved towards her. They looked at the limp child and she thought . . . they know. They know. No one dared to move the baby from her. They stood around her as if guarding her and him from more danger. They did their bit. One woman recognised her.

'It's that English woman. You know. Her husband is doing the Government work in Betws-y-Coed. Shy she is.'

'We must get a message. How do we get in touch with him?'

She knew she must answer. She did not.

The doctor came.

'You must come with us. You must come to the hospital with him. You can carry him if you want.'

A car arrived from somewhere. As she got into it clinging on to him, the letter to her mother fell out of his clothing and fluttered on to the road alongside the wet and muddy leaves. She noticed the ink bleeding across the envelope and then it ceased to claim her attention further.

At the hospital they took him away. They pulled him from her. One nurse held her arms from behind and another prized the bundle away. Her coat was open exposing blood and milk stains. She looked down at herself feeling the cold entering where she was wet. Blood and milk. She remembered the moment of his birth. Blood and white . . .

'Your name please?' said a nurse standing with a form and pen. She opened her mouth but no sound came out.

'Speak up.' said the nurse sharply. There was so much to do, this was irritating. She tried again. No sound.

'It's shock,' said another nurse. 'Go and get that doctor back before he leaves, quick.'

'She is suffering from shock. She needs a sedative . . . to calm her down . . . the husband . . . she won't be able to stay here . . . ask her to write down her name, address and how to get in touch with him . . . need to know the child's name, age, any other information we should know . . .? He's in Ward 5 . . . Yes, head injury . . . not much hope . . . For God's sake get that woman out of here . . . give her something . . . stay with her a while . . .' The voices went in and out of focus. Her throat solidified and froze.

A middle-aged nurse came and held her hand.

'It'll be all right dear. Come on, now. Here's a cup of tea. I've put some sugar in it. It will help you. You've had a shock. It'll be all right, it looks better than we thought at first. You should go home now . . . he's in the best place. He is in the right hands, you mustn't worry yourself about him. That's better.'

Swallowing was almost impossible, there was a constriction. She could only let little sips through.

'You get in touch tomorrow, we'll let you know how he is. You'd better leave some of your milk, if he'll take it that is. Come on. I'll get the breast pump, we can keep your milk in the fridge. There is always other babies that need it . . . had a mother die in childbirth two days ago . . . now, what did you say your name was?'

She again tried to speak but the sounds would not come. She mouthed her name. The nurse turned towards her so that she could stare at her mouth.

'What's that? Margaret? Is that what you are called? Margaret? Yes? Good. Margaret what?' Again she closely watched the mouth.

'Ommm? Margaret Ommalee? No? O, yes? No? O'Malley? Margaret O'Malley? Good.'

When her husband took her home, he talked gently to her and coaxed her to tell him what had happened that day. She tried to talk but her throat had knitted across. It had tightened and hardened so that no sound was possible. Her voice had been left back there in the past.

The child remained in hospital for three weeks. He had been hurt badly, the doctor said, but he had made an amazing recovery. There might be some long-term effects but nothing had surfaced so far. He had to have check-ups every week. Every week she took in a pad and pencil and wrote or signed answers to the questions about the baby's activities. After six months the doctors said he was fine. There was no need for her to bring him back unless he showed unexpected signs that caused her worry. He congratulated her on how bonny the baby was. How strong and healthy and how very, very alert he was. She smiled and was proud. On the way home in the bus he sat on her lap watching her face all the time. She spoke to him constantly. No sound came out of her mouth but he understood every word. He watched her eyes, her hands, her mouth and he responded all the while with the same wordy and agitated silence.

THE NICE BOYS

Isabel Colegate

October 8th

Of course Venice is not the same. How could it be? Last year was the first time, and with Jacob.

There were two nice boys on the train from Milan. I talked to them. I have been through bad periods before I know how easy it is to become isolated if you are unhappy.

I asked them for a light.

The one in the corner brought out a box of matches, lit one, and held it out to me with a steady hand.

'What's that on your arm?' he asked. 'A bite?'

I had taken off my coat, and the sleeves of my dress were short. There was a circular bruise on my forearm.

I explained feebly that I had bitten myself in a temper. The travel agency had muddled all my arrangements just when I was fussing about my packing. 'I know it sounds stupid,' I said. 'But it did calm me down as a matter of fact.'

The boy who had lit my cigarette pushed back the sleeve of his jacket, undid the button of his beautifully white cuff, and showed me his wrist. One side of it was purple and swollen. It was a much more serious bruise than mine.

'That was a bite,' he said.

I wondered what to say.

The other boy said, 'His kid sister did it,' and they both

laughed, excessively I thought, but I suppose they were remembering a funny incident.

'She's a terror,' said the first boy.

'How old is she?' I asked. They told me she was eight and called Jean, and then a noisy Italian family moved into the carriage with a lot of luggage and our conversation came to an end for the time being.

We exchanged another non-committal word or two on the journey, about the weather and this or that, and I was rather struck by them. It was not just that they were nice-looking and well-dressed, with good haircuts and Italian shoes, but that they had a certain air of confidence and reserve as if they already had some achievement to their credit. I don't know what the achievement could be. They might have been pop singers; but there would have been fans, and a manager or something. Academic success? They might have been grammar school boys who had won scholarships somewhere; but no, they had more assurance than that. Anyway, whatever its origin, their air of authority was rather charming.

Of course, all young people are confident these days. Confident, independent, and cool. He didn't sink his teeth into his own flesh at three o'clock in the morning after hours of sobbing and screaming with jealous misery. I wish I had his self-control.

October 12th

I am glad I came. Venice is wonderfully soothing, wonderfully sad.

I remember my very first impression, which was one of gaiety; but that was misleading. I remember going down the Grand Canal in a launch – boats dashing about through the choppy water, the sun on buildings of pure fantasy – it was so active, startling, beautiful, such a glorious joke. I remember standing up and laughing, and Jacob watching me with surprise and pleasure. Later I discovered the Venice I loved best, the Venice of regret.

We stayed for two nights at the Gritti Palace, but then it became obvious that my money was not going to last, and so we moved to this same seedy pensione where I am now, not far from the Accademia bridge. The pale German woman is still the proprietress. She does not remember me, thank goodness. I was right to come. It is easy to be sad here, and when I am sad I am not enraged. Besides, Venice's glory is all over too.

I was rather nervous when I came in. I was afraid she would ask about Jacob. I could not decide whether to deny having been here before, or to say 'He is busy,' or to say 'He has married someone younger, prettier, and richer than I am.' I need not have bothered. She hardly looked at me; but when she saw my English passport she said, 'I see you have more terrible murders in London.' She was not interested in me, only in some idea she had about a gas-lit London where sadistic murderers pad through the fog about their dreadful business: some foreigners do have this picture of London in their minds. I asked her if she had ever been there and she said no. 'It is terrible,' she said. 'These poor girls.' Someone has evidently been chopping up prostitutes again. She seemed to have a morbid interest in the whole business.

When we were here before the sun was shining. This time it is misty and damp. Appropriate, perhaps. Loneliness, damp, melancholy, the seediness of a place from which the glory has fled. I went to Torcello in the water-bus, simply to be on the lagoon again, and visit those dead islands, grass on stone, quiet water over fallen palaces; and felt a sort of happiness. How soon will all Venice slide into the sea?

The boys from the train are staying in the pensione. They were signing themselves in when I came in this evening. I greeted them, and saw that they had written 'N. Bray, S. Brook'. Seeing where I was looking the one who had been writing said with a smile, 'He's Sig. I'm Poney.' Sig is slightly smaller and quieter, Poney darker, more handsome and less intense. They seem unlikely names.

October 15th

The fog has come. Damp cold fog has flopped over Venice, making the whole place mysteriously different. The people seem to accept it with a certain gloomy relish.

They say it is better than the floods they often have at this time of the year.

There is nothing to do. I walk endlessly. Everyone seems to have disappeared: only occasionally another human being pads past in the fog, muffled to the eyes, a stranger. The little restaurant round the corner where I often go for lunch is usually empty, the student waiters have disappeared and only the close-faced husband and wife who own it are there. And the cats. There are always cats in Venice.

I begin to think it may be lucky that I could not keep my room after November the first. Apparently the German woman closes down then and goes for a holiday, to her mother in Munich, she told me. She's an odd woman. She seems to have no family here, or friends. She has struck up some sort of relationship with the two boys. They order her about in a rather disagreeable manner: they are really awfully arrogant, but she seems to like it. There is something slavish in her attitude as she fetches and carries for them.

They have the room next to mine. Last night I was awake until about five. I had taken my last sleeping pill, and when it didn't work I began to panic. I walked up and down, tried to read, did exercises. It was no good. All the agony came back. I am so bloody jealous. It is hardly sane. I hate it, but what can I do? Here she is at that party, leaning against the door – how pleased with her own looks – and Jacob walking towards her, unsteadily because he is a bit drunk, and I recognise with a shock that the curve of her cheek and chin is rather like mine – and I am lost in the endless torture of imagining them together, of remembering his love-making and imagining him making love to her. He said, 'She's awfully sweet really, you'd like her.' Unimaginable cruelty.

At some stage in the night I opened my window and leaned out into the fog. The water of the little canal below slopped gently against its walls. Someone laughed, quite close to me. I shut the window quickly and leant against the wall for a moment. The laugh had come from the next room and had sounded so spiteful that I thought for a moment that the two boys must have been watching me and were laughing at my agony. It was half-past three. I had seen them go upstairs at about eleven. I listened, and could just hear a murmur of voices, then a series of bumps. After a moment I opened the window again very slightly, but I could still only hear the voices without being able to make out what they were saying. Evidently it was not me they were interested in. And then I heard someone cry out 'The King!' in a harsh high voice. 'The King! The King!' Then the laugh again. Then silence. I shut the window.

I don't know what the explanation was. They didn't look in the least tired this morning, which is more than could be said for me. They were talking to Frau Engels when I came down, about the famous London murders again. It was not prostitutes apparently, but a respectable family in a respectable suburb who were found dead in their beds one morning, having all been murdered and mutilated during the night. It does seem extraordinary and horrible. They had no enemies. I imagine Jacob's wife – but no, of course I don't want her to be murdered – sometimes I could be half in love with her in a sort of way. Today I feel sick and tired. Lack of sleep gives me indigestion, my obsession makes me feel guilty: I must try to distract myself, but my will seems hopelessly weak.

I asked Frau Engels about the boys when they had gone.

'They are charming,' I said to start the conversation. 'Are they on holiday?'

'Yes.' She did not seem particularly keen to talk, but I persisted.

'What part of England do they come from?' I asked.

'They are from – what do you call it? – a home,' she said.

'What sort of home?' I asked, startled.

'They are from very distinguished parentage,' she said portentously.

'Oh, yes?' I did not understand.

'They have been supported in this home for orphans by their fathers who were both from high up in the English aristocracy, but who were not married with their mothers.'

'I see. That sort of home. But how have they money? I mean, to buy those clothes and come for holidays in Venice?'

'From their fathers, who gave them much money when they attained eighteen years.'

'But do they know their fathers then?'

'They know, but they cannot tell.'

And then an elderly Italian couple who were staying in the pensione came up to ask whether it was not possible to stay after November the first: their daughter was joining them and they hoped the weather might have improved by then.

'It is impossible, I am so very sorry, but on the first I must everything close.' She gave her remote correct smile, and I walked out into the fog.

In order to reach the vaporetto stop I had to cross the small canal which ran beside the pensione, and as I turned across the little humped bridge, the boys materialised out of the fog and crossed with me, one on each side. They did not speak at first, and nor did I. Finally Sig said, in a mild conversational tone, 'What were you talking to the old bag about?'

'Frau Engels?' I said. 'We were talking about you as a matter of fact.'

'What did she say?' asked Sig.

'She said she believed you were both orphans.'

They laughed. Sig's is the high, hard laugh, the other is a kind of low giggle, rather sexy: it struck me that neither sounded genuinely amused.

'She's just a stupid old bag,' said Sig. 'She fancies Poney, that's all.'

'She'd like to eat me,' said Poney, in a bored sort of way.

'Hardly the verb I'd have chosen,' said Sig. They talk in a semi-facetious; slangy, private joke sort of way which is often awkward. I suppose that may be how schoolboys talk, I don't know.

'Aren't you orphans then?' I asked.

'We come from respectable middle-class backgrounds,' said Sig. 'We live in Epping, my dear, that respectable middle-class suburb where you may be chopped into little pieces as you lie a-sleeping.'

'We were so frightened we ran away from home,' said Poney in a baby voice. 'We were afraid of the nasty man with the chopper. We suck our thumbs you see.'

'Where are you going?' asked Sig as I slowed down.

'I am going to look at the pictures here,' I said, turning towards the Accademia. 'There's nothing much else to do in the fog is there?'

'Do you know one of these palaces is for sale?' said Sig.

'I had heard it was.'

'We're thinking of buying it,' said Sig casually.

'But you must be millionaires!'

'Oh, we're all right for money,' said Sig. 'Cheery-bye.' They glided away into the fog.

I can't make up my mind whether they are ridiculous or offensive. They would be ridiculous but for something peculiar about their partnership. I don't know whether it is a homosexual relationship or not: it might be that that makes them seem so close, so set apart from the common run of men.

October 21st

I cannot sleep. And the fog is still here.

Last night two girls appeared for dinner at the pensione. The boys were out, but everyone else was there, that is to say, the elderly Italian couple, the two moderately attractive French sisters and the daughter of one of them, the solitary Italian who looks like some sort of minor businessman, and myself. That, with the boys, is the sum of the guests at the moment. An Italian brother and sister who live next door do the waiting, and Frau Engels herself cooks.

The girls were nice-looking and well dressed. They spoke with American accents. One was dark and curly-haired, the other wore glasses but had quite good features. They both wore little hats. They immediately drew attention to themselves by being appallingly rude. They complained loudly of the dreary decor before they went in to dinner. At dinner they ordered the waiter about most disagreeably and soon sent for Frau Engels herself in order to complain of the food. It annoyed me intensely to see how she took it from them, padding backwards and forwards with a cringing anxiety to please, quite different from her usual frosty attitude towards her guests.

I finished my meal as quickly as I could and went

upstairs. I had not been there long before I heard someone going into the next room, and the sound of voices and laughter. I decided to go and read downstairs. As I passed the boys' room the door opened. Frau Engels came out laughing and carrying some clothes. Behind her I caught a glimpse of Sig, still half-dressed, in women's clothes.

As soon as I saw it I wondered why I had not realised before that the American girls were in fact Sig and Poney. All the same the transformation had been alarmingly convincing. I didn't really like it. I didn't like the way they had abused her and she had cringed. I didn't like their pleasure in having deceived us all. There was no question of throwing off the disguise and allowing us to share the joke: there they were in the bedroom laughing at us. I don't like them. I don't know why I ever thought they were nice boys. I think there is something unpleasant about them.

October 24th

Sinus trouble back at its very worst. A constant headache that nothing seems to cure. I don't know why I don't leave. My will seems to have been weakened by the lowering insinuations of the soggy fog: why doesn't it go? I wander and wander, waiting for the fog to clear and the sun to come out. I have nothing in my head, no thought, no will, nothing. Except pain. I wander, and lean over bridges, and watch the slack water. Pain pain go away. Come again another day. Immeasurable pain. Last night my dreaming soul was king again.

I hate those boys. They shouted again last night, something about the king. I think they have orgies up there night after night. There's something suspicious about the way they are always so clean. Only guilty people wash as much as they do.

Also they are morbid. They came in this morning as I was drinking coffee in the dreary little sitting-room, and sat down beside me. They were carrying newspapers.

'Haven't caught him yet, I see,' said Sig.

'Caught who?' I asked.

'This murderer.'

'Oh.'

'Aren't you interested then?' asked Poney.

'Not particularly,' I said.

'Don't you think there's something about it though?' said Poney encouragingly. 'I mean these people lying there safe in their snug little beds in their snug little house, and suddenly bash, bash, they're all in pieces?' He gave his rather charming boyish smile. 'Not interesting?'

I smiled feebly, too tired to talk to them.

Sig laughed his nasty laugh and Poney's smile widened. 'That'll teach them, won't it?' he said.

'Teach them what?' I said.

'Teach them who's master,' said Poney quietly.

'He who wields the axe,' said Sig.

'Ah,' said Poney. 'He must have been a great man all right, that killer, don't you think so?'

'No,' I said flatly.

'Don't you like us?' said Sig suddenly.

'Good Heavens I – I hardly know you,' I said, embarrassed.

'At first you seemed to like us,' Sig went on, watching me intently. 'Now you don't seem so friendly. Do we offend you?'

'No, no, of course not.'

'But there is something about us you find yourself resenting? Have you ever tried hypnosis? For your headaches I mean?'

'How did you know I have headaches?'

'I can see. Have you ever been hypnotised?' He was staring at me much too hard.

'No,' I said.

'I should think you'd be a bad subject,' he said, leaning back in his chair.

'Sig could do it,' said Poney confidently.

'I could. But no one else. She'd withstand anyone else. What is it about us that annoys you?'

'I think you're talking nonsense. I'm not annoyed by you.'

He was leaning forward again. 'Is it that you feel the power coming from us?'

'Power?'

'That you feel we're in some way set apart.'

'You seem to feel that yourselves. I had noticed that.'

'Do you know what sets us apart?' said Sig very quietly. His gaze had become unbearably intense by now. 'Do you know what it is? Our *virtue*.'

A moment's peculiar silence. And then they both noticeably relaxed, and laughed briefly, and looked like two prankish schoolboys.

I can't make them out.

October 27th

A horrible day.

It started well. The fog had cleared and the sun was shining. Everything seemed to have changed. My headache was no better, but I felt calmer, convalescent almost. I took the vaporetto to San Marco and sat in the Piazza to have some coffee. The place was quite crowded; everyone seemed to have gathered there to see Venice reborn.

I saw the boys moving in my direction, and sat back behind my paper hoping they would pass: but they had seen me, and paused, though they did not sit down.

'Got them yet?' Poney asked, gesturing slightly towards my paper.

'Got what?' I said.

'The murderers.'

I wondered vaguely why he used the plural.

'It doesn't say so,' I said. 'Lovely morning, isn't it?'

'More like it, isn't it?' agreed Poney. 'We're off to that crooked old house agent again,' and they walked off through the tables, neat, spruce, untouchable.

Then in the evening there was a question of moving some furniture. Frau Engels was making preparations for shutting up her house and wanted, for some reason, to move several pieces of furniture from downstairs up into one of the empty bedrooms. There were several chairs, three Viennese-looking cabinets, and a big mahogany cupboard. She asked the boys to help her. Seriously they removed their well-cut jackets, rolled up the sleeves of their impeccably clean white shirts, and set to work. They lifted the heavy furniture with no difficulty at all; and I saw the muscles in their arms. The two Frenchwomen and the daughter of one of them were coming in at the time, and were much impressed.

'But how is it you do this?' one of the Frenchwomen asked them. 'You are weight-lifters?'

'It's nothing really,' said Poney.

'It's a matter of training,' said Sig, remotely.

'But you do this training for what?' she asked. 'You are athletes?'

'We just keep in training,' said Sig.

'You never know when it may come in useful,' said Poney.

They went on with their work. The Frenchwomen passed them admiringly and went upstairs. The boys began showing off, to each other more than to anyone else.

Poney flexed his muscles and lifted a small chair, pretending it was a great weight.

'The strong man,' said Sig. 'Nothing he can't do.'

'You're not bad yourself,' said Poney. 'Come on, let's see those muscles now.'

Sig lifted one of the little cabinets which really did look heavy. Poney put down his chair and lifted the pair of cabinets. They stood side by side swaying slightly, then gently lowered the weights without faltering in their control.

'Not bad, not bad,' said Poney again.

'You're the best,' said Sig, who was breathing rather heavily. 'You're the king of the weight-lifters.'

'You could lift a heavy man.'

'You could hold one down.'

'You know your judo.'

'You could lift a heavy axe.'

'You could have gone into that house in Woodbridge Road. You could have dealt with that fat family.'

'You could have wielded that axe.'

'You could have taken it in turns with me.'

'You could have smothered the parents.'

'You could have despatched the two girls, wham, wham, all gone.'

'You could have swung that axe.'

'You could have swopped their heads . . .' Here Poney became lost in his low giggle. Sig joined in. They bent over the furniture, laughing. Then each taking one side of one of the cabinets, they began to carry it towards the stairs.

'Ah, we could have swung it,' said Sig, calm after his laughter.

'We could have swung it,' echoed Poney in his deeper voice.

And suddenly I knew that they had.

They were murderers.

With absolute certainty and terror, I knew that they were murderers.

'You are not well?' Frau Engels was looking at me strangely.

'Oh, yes, I – I have a bit of a headache.' I did not dare to say more because I felt certain that she would think me mad. Besides, she was so strangely fascinated by the boys. Unless she knew already, and this was the secret of their relationship? Or perhaps she merely sensed in them a depth of evil which appealed to some perverted leaning of her own? She offered me aspirin. I refused, but asked if she had any back numbers of English papers. She led me to a cupboard and left me to look for what I wanted.

I soon found it. I read everything I could see about the Epping murders. A family of four, father, mother, and two daughters had been found dead and mutilated. The crime was described as being of appalling brutality. No one had seen or heard a thing. They had lived in a detached house in its own garden in a high-class suburban street. They had had no enemies. The father had worked in a City office, the two girls had been to a local school, were popular at the tennis club, and looked quite pretty from the photographs. There were interviews with the various young friends – no, Jean and Pam had no special boyfriends, everybody had liked them, Jean was on the committee of the tennis club, Pam was keener on riding, they were the most popular girls in the neighbourhood. The parents went to Church, the mother was a member of the local Women's Institute. Here was something. And yet I was hardly surprised to read it. 'Mrs Bray, Chairman of the local branch, said at her home in nearby Forest Avenue, that Mrs Anderson had been a regular attender at W.I. Meetings. "It hardly bears thinking of," she said.'

Poney's name was Bray. I had seen him writing it in the Register when they first arrived.

Before dinner I found them sitting in the tiny bar next to the dining-room drinking fruit juice (they never touch alcohol). It was an effort to go and sit beside them, but I made it.

'Whereabouts in Epping do you live?' I began, ordering whisky. 'I used to know it slightly.'

'Forest Avenue,' said Poney. 'We both do.'

'Isn't that quite near where the murder was?'

'I thought you weren't interested in the murder,' said Sig.

'I'm not particularly,' I said. 'But it becomes more interesting if you knew the people.'

'We didn't,' said Sig firmly.

I did not dare to pursue it. Their faces had become closed and uninformative. Poney patted his already immaculately tidy hair and said, 'I wonder what's for jolly old dins.'

'How are you getting on with your house-hunting?' I asked.

'We've gone off it,' said Poney. 'It seems you can't rely on the weather here. We're going to Sardinia in a few days to look around there.'

'Was anything stolen from the house where the murder was?' I asked before I could stop myself.

'Hey, what's the . . .' began Poney, but Sig interrupted him.

He said very clearly, 'Some valuable jewellery I believe.'

'What's the big interest suddenly?' said Poney.

'Oh, I don't know,' I said. 'Tell me about Sardinia. I believe it's lovely there.'

'So old Aga Khan says,' said Poney, stroking his hair again. 'He's looking out a decent plot for us.'

Then the bell went for dinner.

I don't know what to do.

It is late now and I have locked myself into my bedroom. My headache has come back and I cannot sleep. I can just hear their voices next door. They talk so much alone in their room. What do they do in there?

They have some horrible thing between them. I felt it from the beginning. They are linked by some fantasy they have built up about power and violence, I am sure of it. Perhaps the girls snubbed them at a local dance. One of the girls was called Jean. Didn't they tell me that was the name of Poney's little sister, when he was showing me his bruise from a bite? Jean. I'm sure they said Jean. Perhaps they simply chose the Anderson family because they were so obviously harmless. This made it more of a joke, a clever trick. They enjoy fooling people; as they enjoyed letting us all think they were two American girls the other night, to score off the rest of the world, to build up their sense of isolation and superiority. I suppose they are mad, if to live in a world of fantasy is mad; or perhaps Sig is mad and Poney merely bad, and utterly corrupted. Heaven knows what appalling rituals may be going on in the next room even now – that shout of 'The King!' – what shall I do if I hear it again tonight? But what can I do? Who would believe me? I have no friends in Venice. Frau Engels is useless. What about the other people in the pensione? Those unimaginative-looking Frenchwomen with the daughter, the bored businessman, the doddering old couple – what use would they be? I can't go to the British Consul unless I can offer something more positive than just my own conviction. In a way the people I know best, though only in the most casual way, are the couple who run the little restaurant round the corner, Mario and his wife. I don't even particularly like them, but we have talked a certain amount. I think I will try and say something to them tomorrow. In the meantime I can do nothing but sit behind my locked door and listen to the murmurs and occasional bumps from the next room.

October 29th

I think I did hear the shout, but it may have been a dream. I took three sleeping pills. It was too many and I have felt terrible all day.

I lunched at the restaurant. I said to Mario, 'Do you ever see those two young English boys who are staying at my pensione?'

'Yes, they have been in once or twice,' he answered in his

good English. 'Architectural students, they told me. They seemed nice boys. I lent them a guide book.'

'They are not architectural students,' I said.

He looked surprised.

'They lie to everyone, they live in a complete fantasy,' I said. 'Look, if I tell you something, will you take it seriously, will you give me your advice?'

He said he would, and sat down at my table, looking worried.

It was difficult to go on.

'I have reason to believe,' I said. 'In fact I know, that they have committed a terrible crime.'

He looked down at the table cloth in silence. I felt I was doing badly.

'I know it sounds absurd,' I said. 'But I am quite sure about this. I wouldn't say so otherwise. You must believe me.'

But he didn't. He listened politely as I told him of my suspicions, and then he told me that he thought I was mistaken.

'When the fog comes I sometimes have strange ideas myself. You told me you had been having sinus trouble and bad headaches. You don't think you could be mistaken about these boys?'

'I know I am not mistaken.'

But I could see it was no good. All I could do was to make him say that if at any stage I needed help I could come to him.

'But of course,' he said, standing up with obvious relief. 'We are your friends.'

During the day I managed to see the Frenchwomen and the elderly couple. I asked them whether they thought there was anything odd about the boys. They all said no, they thought them charming. I did not go on.

I do not know what to do. They might do it again, kill someone I mean.

October 31st

I notice them more now. I notice the black hairs on the back of Poney's hands, and the tight line between the eyebrows on Sig's white face. I notice how they both have the same strutting walk, how close they walk and how they never touch. I notice the metallic tone in Sig's voice, the sleepy softness in Poney's. I notice how light they are on their feet, how controlled; and yet I've seen, in Sig's eyes only and only when he is looking at Poney, an occasional doubt. I think this must be when the veil of fantasy momentarily twitches. I don't think Poney doubts. He has been handed his myth and he is living it out.

I watch them. I think they are watching me. I want to go, but I must stay. They are bound to make some move, and then I can send for help and run away myself. But I can't leave them, knowing what I do. I am not yet so disgusted with the human race. They must be caught, and stopped.

What will they do? I lurk about the pensione, pretending to read, watching them. The other guests look at me oddly, wondering what I am doing, but I can't talk, not yet. I feel ill and desperately anxious.

November 2nd

And now it is all over.

The next morning I followed them in the Piazza and sat down a few tables away to drink some coffee. A girl whom I knew slightly in London came up to speak to me. She said that some friends of hers, with whom she was staying, were giving a party that night after dinner. Would I like to come?

I had not seen anyone from London for some time. Indeed for the last few days I had had no conversation except with other people at the pensione. I said I would go to the party.

Later when I was in my bedroom changing I heard the voices of the boys and Frau Engels in the next room. I opened the window and leaned out. I heard Frau Engels sobbing, 'No,' and the two voices together, one high and one low, repeating, 'Yes, yes, yes, yes.'

I finished changing quickly and went downstairs. What else could I do? What could I tell to whom? Who would be concerned to know what went on in a bedroom between a middle-aged proprietress of the pensione and her two young lodgers: who would do more than shrug knowingly?

I stayed late at the party. Not so much because it was a good party as because I did not want to go back to the pensione. It was a boring party really. My friend's friends were stuffy Italians who lived in a comfortable little flat at the top of a fine flaking palazzo. One or two of the other people there looked quite interesting, but my Italian was not good enough to find out whether the impression was misleading, and I spent most of the evening talking to an American professor and his wife. I almost forgot about the boys, but not quite. I stayed until I was too tired to stay any longer. Then I walked out into the damp darkness. The vaporetto was still running. I got off at the Accademia bridge and walked towards the pensione, along the narrow way between the houses, over the little canal and up to the door. It was open. No one was at the desk. There was a light on the stairs, none in the hall.

I moved quietly towards the stairs. There was a sound above me. I stopped. There was silence. I went on. Another soft dragging sound, very slight. I went on. The weak bulb revealed the landing much as usual, shadowy, the faded Turkish carpet, the row of doors, mine, theirs, the Frenchwomen's, the couple's, the businessman's: Frau Engels slept on the top floor.

The faint sound seemed to come from the businessman's room. There were shoes outside some of the doors, ready for the maid to clean when she came in in the morning – the two Frenchwomen's and the daughter's, and the elderly couple's – there were none outside the businessman's door, or the boys', or mine. There were long shadows beside the shoes. They were not shadows. They were marks. Something had been spilt. But beside all the shoes? I moved closer. All the shoes had a long dark stain coming from them. They were neatly placed outside the doors but surrounded by this dark wet stain. But the shoes were not empty. They had feet in them. There was a lot of blood.

A handle turned quietly. The businessman's door opened very slightly. A hand came out holding a pair of shoes. It placed them neatly outside the door.

I ran, stumbling on the stairs.

I battered on the door of the restaurant.

At last they came.

'It's happened. They've done it again. They've killed everyone in the pensione.'

'All right. Steady now. Come in.'

Mario and his wife were both there, in their night-clothes, looking startled, and then annoyed. I saw the beginnings of disbelief on their faces and for the first time in my life I collapsed into hysterics.

They slapped my face, made me swallow several pills, and put me to bed. I kept begging them to hurry, to get the police, to go round there before it was too late. They promised they would, and left me. I must have been quite heavily drugged because I fell asleep almost immediately.

And in the morning, unbelievably, they had done nothing.

I woke, heavy-headed, at nine o'clock, dressed as quickly as I could and went downstairs. They were in the kitchen drinking coffee.

'What happened?' I said.

The wife did not look at me. Mario said quite kindly, 'You had a nightmare.'

'But the police . . .?'

'We didn't want to wake them in the middle of the night. Now come and have some coffee.'

I made a great effort and remained calm.

'Please will you come round there with me now.'

Mario came.

The pensione seemed very quiet as we approached. The front door was still open. We walked into the dim hall. A figure moved slowly towards us from the kitchen door. It was Frau Engels. Her face was very white except for where several raw red scratches ran down one side of it.

'Good morning, Frau Engels,' said Mario, in English for my sake. 'Have you had an accident?'

'It was in the fog. I walked into a tree,' she said brusquely. 'Have you come to collect your luggage, madame?'

But I had already passed her without answering and was rushing up the stairs. The stairs were still there. I burst into the boys' room. It was empty. Their clothes and luggage had gone. I went into the next room, and the next. They were all empty. There was no sign of anyone.

Frau Engels and Mario had followed me up the stairs. I confronted them.

'Where are they?' I said. 'Where are the boys?'

'They left this morning,' she said, looking at me with the oddest hatred. 'Everybody left this morning.'

'Why?'

'It is November the 1st. I told you. I am closing down.'

'These stains . . .'

She explained them away. She said they were varnish, which had run when the wooden boards had been stained brown. I tried to insist that they should send for the police and have the stains tested to prove that they were blood. I asked where the two servants were, but Frau Engels said they had already left for a holiday with their family in Naples. I heard Mario murmur to her in Italian that he would telephone for a doctor.

'I go to get the police,' he said to me soothingly as he turned to go downstairs.

'No,' I said. 'I'll take my luggage now and come back later with the British Consul.'

I packed and left. I went to the hotel where my acquaintance from London was staying. I found her and told her my story. I took her with me back to the pensione. It was locked and shuttered. Frau Engels had left.

It is of course an impossible story. I can hardly blame people for not wanting to believe it. Only I know it is true. I am not a hysterical or deluded person.

Frau Engels also knows that I know that it is true. I do not know to what extent she was involved or whether her appalling association with the boys is still going on, but it seems likely that she may somehow or other have told them about my return to the pensione.

This is the horror with which I have to live.

They will find me. One day I shall take a train. I shall settle myself in my corner seat, open the paperback I have bought to read on the journey. And I shall look up. And there will be two nice boys sitting opposite me.

RECIPE FOR VICTORY

Maeve Binchy

She always knew when he was starting a new affair. He spoke more quickly, for one thing; there was an intensity about things that normally didn't matter at all as if some kind of scales had fallen from his eyes. This time he burned indignantly about a planning permission that should never have been granted, and ten minutes later about the way RTE had arranged its summer schedules. When he began to speak his mind on litter bins being uglier than the litter they were meant to contain Rona knew that the affair had begun.

There was no problem in knowing who the affair was *with*. Aengus was so predictable. He didn't seem able to find lovers for himself all on his own. He picked them from amongst his wife's friends. Or that's what he had done on the previous occasions. The previous *three* occasions.

For a while Rona had tried having no friends. Or not letting him meet her friends. But with young children that was difficult; there were school runs, there were the children's parties, there were neighbours. She couldn't impose this kind of isolation on herself just in case. Just in case it happened again. And anyway friends were a huge consolation, it would be insane to deny yourself the company and support of women throughout your life, just because there were a few rotten apples in every barrel. False friends, wives ripe for the flattery and the buzzy adventure of a little fling.

Rona couldn't imagine it herself. All that juvenile

seventeen-year-old business of wondering would he ring, keeping it a secret despite speaking glances. It had been hard enough keeping things secret from her mother. Fancy having to keep things a secret from your husband. And your children.

And that is exactly what her friend Finn had to do these days. Make up fictitious shopping trips, convincing explanations of why the car should be parked in unlikely places, give reasons why she couldn't be at the school's sale of work. And Finn worked part-time as well. How did she do it, Rona wondered. She was surprised at herself for the detached way she was able to think about it. Almost as if she were up in the air looking down on the feverish activity of mortals below. Like you look at ants and wonder mildly what on earth they are doing.

Finn was pretty in what Rona's mother would have called a flashy sort of way. She didn't wear an ankle bracelet but you felt that any moment she might. She had never danced on a table in their presence but there were overtones of table dancing in the way she talked. She was new to the area, married to George, a megabore who saw everything in terms of money and value. Even those who had been enthusiastic followers of property prices in the neighbourhood said that a lot of the interest had fallen out of it once George got hold of the conversation and ran with it. Fortunately for everyone, George wasn't around much, to dominate the barbecues and tell them where they could have got the equipment at half the price. George was away making still more money a lot of the time. Which was fortunate for his wife Finn since she didn't have to listen to him and apologise for him, and indeed have to explain to him what she was doing with Rona's handsome husband Aengus.

It was easy to understand why anyone would be drawn to Aengus. He had deep dark eyes that seemed to look right into your soul. After twelve years of marriage Rona knew that Aengus was often thinking of something very prosaic indeed like how to get a game of golf in on Thursday or whether he had paid the television licence or not. It was just a bonus that he looked so beautifully broody. And of course Rona loved him terribly, just like the women before her time had loved him, and the three women after her marriage. And now Finn. Rona had a set of rules to work to by now. If something happens four times in twelve years you learn how to cope with it.

First: she must refuse to think of him in bed with Finn. The thought must simply not be allowed to enter into her mind. If it did she would become so hurt and betrayed that a great wave of longing would sweep over her. She would cower somewhere like a wounded animal whimpering and railing against a life that had allowed this to happen.

Second: she must develop an easy, on-going friendship with Finn, making it easy for Aengus to bring her name into the conversation. Rona noticed that when men were in love they always wanted to talk about the loved one, no matter how banal the observation. If Finn were a regular visitor to the home it would be easier and less contrived for him to dredge up references to her.

Third: she must look out for warning signs that Finn was about to confess everything and head her off at the pass. The great danger in things like this was in letting matters get out into the open. It was almost impossible to cope with something which had been allowed the indulgence and the momentum of being acknowledged. On the two occasions when Finn had begun to look tearful and confiding, Rona changed the mood and the subject with such speed that it even impressed her herself.

There was a different way of dealing with everyone. Rona knew that you had to play to your own strengths and to the enemy's weakness. Or some kind of phrase like that. She had heard it around the time of the first infidelity, the year she had to dislodge the ice-cool blonde Camilla. Rona's strength had been sailing, she had discovered that Camilla's weakness had been in the same area, she was a woman whose legs buckled and whose stomach heaved when off dry land. Rona had arranged the outing, Camilla had believed the 'calm as a mill pond, really just like a sheet of glass' argument that was presented. To this day Rona remembered with some pleasure the retching, the red eyes, the clinging to Aengus, the oh-my-God wails, the near public revelation of past sins in front of everyone including Camilla's husband.

It hadn't been hard really. It was merely a question of waiting for the right opportunity. As with the others. You could study somebody very well, if the person hadn't an idea you were in there investigating weaknesses. All you had to do was to keep calm, and ignore the signs of embarrassment. Most women, even women who had affairs with your husband, were not ruthless. They felt awkward accepting your kindness and welcome, they would prefer to distance themselves from you as they wrapped themselves closer around your husband. You must prevent the former if you were ever going to stop the latter.

Finn, it turned out, was a great sailor, no mileage to be gained there. In a superficial sort of way she was well up in books and theatres, there would be no point in trying to expose her as an ignoramus. She went out to work and was successful as a businesswoman open to no charges of being a Mrs Feather. She shared none of the unacceptable money obsessions that made her husband George so unwelcome in their set. Finn was open and straightforward, at least up the point where she had committed herself to someone else's husband. Rona would have to work on her quite a bit to identify where the weaknesses lay.

Because of Rule One, about never allowing any image of their lovemaking to come within yards of her, Rona found it easy to entertain her husband's mistress. She even found Finn good company when she dropped in for a drink on her way home from work. Finn's children, two dark handsome boys, seemed to be very well able to look after themselves.

'I don't believe in mollycoddling them too much. They have to grow up to be big strong men,' Finn said, looking at Rona as she spoke, but really talking to Aengus. She lingered over the words 'big strong men'. Rona could see her husband fingering his collar nervously. Oh, knowledge is power, Rona thought to herself and wondered, just for a moment, why her mind seemed to be full of little clichés and catchphrases and sayings. Maxims that must have been used a thousand times by other people, and always seemed mint-new to her.

'But don't you think it's the one area where men are utterly hopeless?' Rona was conspiratorial, taking Finn into her confidence as if Aengus was not there. 'I'm all for preserving the mystique of cookery, letting them think they couldn't get on without us.'

'I think they'd find it pretty difficult all right.' Finn still addressed the words to Rona but the flirtation went straight across the kitchen to Aengus.

Rona stood happily amid her shining copper pans and her little kingdom. She smiled as if nothing was amiss.

'I don't know, I feel men would starve if you left them alone, they invented all kinds of complicated can openers to make life easier . . . but apart from great chefs and a very few men you don't see them, experimenting, or being interested in cooking do you . . .? Does George, for example?'

Rona saw to her satisfaction that Aengus frowned at the name of George. Good.

Finn didn't frown. 'George is hardly any example of anything,' she said lightly. 'He is a law unto himself, as people say. He's such a workaholic he hardly notices what's put before him. Just gobbles it up.'

From anyone's recollection of George at any gathering this was true. He regarded eating as a necessary interruption in laying down the law.

'That's hard when you go to trouble preparing things.' Rona's murmur was sympathetic but her eyes were sharp. She had a quick stir of excitement. She might be about to discover Finn's weakness. It could be an important moment.

'Oh, I don't do a great deal . . .' Finn began. Rona didn't even have time to show the sympathetic look of surprise she had been planning. Aengus rushed in defensively.

'Come on now, Finn, don't put yourself down, what about that gorgeous pecan pie you were serving when I dropped in to leave those leaflets for George the other night . . . it was entirely yummy.'

Rona smiled a grim smile. Yummy indeed. Dropping in leaflets for George no less. Pecan pie out of a deep freeze in a supermarket, obviously. Would Finn admit it? She held her breath.

'Oh, that was only a simple thing,' Finn said, blushing prettily.

'It tasted great. I don't know how to describe it.' Aengus was a loyal, proud friend. Rona looked at him in a mixture of rage and scorn.

Before either of them could say 'Yummy' again, Rona broke in. 'Aengus loves his food, surest way to his heart, Finn. It must have been some pie. How did you get those pecan nuts – I tried everywhere?'

Finn had all the confidence of a Queen for a Day. 'Just lucky I suppose,' she said. She spoke to Rona. But her words had a meaning for Aengus.

Rona felt she was in charge of the situation; all she must remember was not to try to score cheap points too soon. Don't win any minor battles and lose the war. There would be no silly games proving how little Finn knew about cooking. That might easily make Aengus feel protective. No, indeed, much more subtle methods were called for.

Next evening, Finn called in and Aengus was not there. Rona realised that they must have met during the afternoon, a lovers' snatched hour. Where could they have gone? They wouldn't have dared go to a hotel. The car was too uncomfortable. She mustn't guess because going down that road meant breaking Rule One, it meant making an image of the two of them together. Yet she knew that they had been together. She had needed to ring Aengus and he was out on a call. She rang Finn's office and heard the same message.

Never mind. She was launched on the slow process of breaking up this romance, of ending this affair. She must just get on with it as methodically as she would have approached any other job.

They talked of cooking, the small, freckled, determined Rona and the wild, laughing, abandoned-looking Finn. On and on she prattled, the seemingly innocent deceived wife telling all her husband's favourite dishes, and how he liked them made.

'He's such a baby,' Rona said affectionately. 'He hates to hear how things are made and what goes into them. Just loves the effect, he said. I've long stopped trying to get him to take an interest in ingredients.'

She saw her rival sipping a glass of cold white wine, lips pursed around the glass. For a moment a wild feeling of rage came over Rona. She would like to have smashed the glass from Finn's hand, she would like to have taken a ladle of some scalding liquid and poured it on the tanned shoulders in their skimpy top. But she told herself in that slow measured voice that spoke in her head that this was not the way she could win the war.

Bit by bit, with contempt for Finn, she taught her rival the fine arts of cooking. She never pretended she was teaching her, of course, it was all in the way you said it. 'How do you make a roux, Finn? With cornflour, is it?' she looked interested and helpful and before Finn could stammer anything, Rona had it made.

Whenever she was sure that Finn actually *could* make something she encouraged her to do it. 'Shall I make a raspberry coulis, do you think? Aengus does so love it and it's terribly simple . . . listen could you just do one for me . . . super.'

As the weeks went on she knew that Finn was making mouthwatering little delicacies for Aengus to be served . . . it didn't matter when they were served. Don't think about those cheese straws that Aengus would love if served fresh and with an ice-cold champagne. In bed. Don't think of them together. Keep on and on.

Rona knew that Finn was uneasy about how generous the wronged wife was being. Sometimes she saw a look of contrition on the dark, gypsy-like face. But it was easy to change her mood. Together the two women planned wonderful meals for the unworthy Aengus, but it was never acknowledged that Finn had served him any of the recipes that she learned eagerly, knowing how much he loved good food.

The lovers had planned a weekend away. Aengus called it a conference. Finn called it seeing about schools for the boys. Rona realised it was one of those idyllic cottages where she would love to have spent a happy relaxing weekend with Aengus. No children, just the two of them. But now it would be Aengus and Finn. Even their names sounded good together, she thought, with a suspicion of a tear. But she would not fall at the last fence.

Finn was bubbling with enthusiasm. 'I feel much more confident about cooking since I met you, Rona,' she said in a burst of gratitude.

'No, no,' she protested, 'You were always very good. Look at that wonderful duxelle you taught me.'

'Surely you taught it to me?' Finn was confused.

'No, we were discussing it, you know, how the mushrooms and the onions are chopped so finely . . . all that.'

'But you said it was something Aengus loved?'

'It is, he often orders a chicken duxelle in a restaurant but I never managed to make . . .'

'So you never made it for him?' The gypsy eyes were bright.

'Never.' Rona sounded apologetic almost. But her heart was soaring. The trap had been set.

She held him to her tenderly, the lying husband who was going away to a rented cottage with a gypsy and not to the conference that he had told his wife he was heading for.

She held him in the knowledge that he would be very ill. His allergy to mushrooms was real and had never been mentioned to Finn. Lovers don't talk of allergies which bring on vomiting and diarrhoea. Lovers' wives certainly don't warn faithless Finns.

If she had given him something that looked like a mushroom, Aengus would have refused it. He would never spot it until it was too late, hidden in a duxelle.

He wouldn't leave this new love just because she had prepared food which made him vomit. Aengus wasn't that kind of man.

But the golden edge would have been taken off the affair. The aura of romance would have blown away. Aengus would return to his wife again. To Rona who would welcome him back without ever pretending he had gone.

She smiled to herself, a tired smile. She could do it the next time and the next time. For years to come maybe. Or until she lost interest and didn't care enough any more. Whichever came first.

THE FLOWERS THAT BLOOM IN THE SPRING

Julian Symons

The outsider, Bertie Mays was fond of saying, sees most of the game. In the affair of the Purchases and the visiting cousin from South Africa he saw quite literally all of it. And the end was enigmatic and a little frightening, at least as seen through Bertie's eyes. It left him with the question whether there had been a game at all.

Bertie had retired early from his unimportant and uninteresting job in the Ministry of Welfare. He had a private income, he was unmarried, and his only extravagance was a passion for travel, so why go on working? Bertie gave up his London flat and settled down in the cottage in the Sussex countryside which he had bought years earlier as a weekend place. It was quite big enough for a bachelor, and Mrs Last from the village came in two days a week to clean the place. Bertie himself was an excellent cook.

It was a fine day in June when he called next door to offer Sylvia Purchase a lift to the tea party at the Hall. She was certain to have been asked, and he knew that she would need a lift because he had seen her husband Jimmy putting a case into the boot of their ancient Morris. Jimmy was some sort of freelance journalist, and often went on trips, leaving Sylvia on her own. Bertie, who was flirtatious by nature, had asked if she would like him to keep her company, but she did not seem responsive to the suggestion. Linton House, which the Purchases had rented furnished a few months earlier, was a rambling old place with oak beams and low ceilings. There was an attractive garden, some of which lay between the house and Bertie's cottage, and by jumping over the fence between them Bertie could walk across this garden. He did so that afternoon, taking a quick peek into the sitting-room as he went by. He could never resist such peeks, because he always longed to know what people might be doing when they thought that nobody was watching. On this occasion the sitting-room was empty. He found Sylvia in the kitchen, washing dishes in a half-hearted way.

'Sylvia, you're not ready.' She had on a dirty old cardigan with the buttons done up wrongly. Bertie himself was, as always, dressed very suitably for the occasion in a double-breasted blue blazer with brass buttons, fawn trousers and a neat bow tie. He always wore bow ties, which he felt gave a touch of distinction and individuality.

'Ready for what?'

'Has the Lady of the Manor not bidden you to tea?' That was his name for Lady Hussey up at the Hall.

She clapped hand to forehead, leaving a slight smudge. 'I'd forgotten all about it. Don't think I'll go, can't stand those bun fights.'

'But I have called specially to collect you. Let me be your chauffeur. Your carriage awaits.' Bertie made a sketch of a bow, and Sylvia laughed. She was a blonde in her early thirties, attractive in a slapdash sort of way.

'Bertie, you are a fool. All right, give me five minutes.'

The women may call Bertie Mays a fool, Bertie thought, but how they adore him.

'Oh,' Sylvia said. She was looking behind Bertie, and when he turned he saw a man standing in the shadow of the door. At first glance he thought it was Jimmy, for the man was large and square like Jimmy, and had the same gingery fair colouring. But the resemblance went no further, for as the man stepped forward he saw that their features were not similar.

'This is my cousin Alfred Wallington. He's paying us a visit from South Africa. Our next-door neighbour, Bertie Mays.'

'Pleased to meet you.' Bertie's hand was firmly gripped.

The two men went into the sitting-room, and Bertie asked whether this was Mr Wallington's first visit.

'By no means. I know England pretty well. The south, anyway.'

'Ah, business doesn't take you up north?' Bertie thought of himself as a tactful but expert interrogator, and the question should have brought a response telling him Mr Wallington's occupation. In fact, however, the other man merely said that was so.

'In the course of my work I used to correspond with several firms in Cape Town,' Bertie said untruthfully. Wallington did not comment. 'Is your home near there?'

'No.'

The negative was so firm that it gave no room for further conversational manoeuvre. Bertie felt slightly cheated. If the man did not want to say where he lived in South Africa of course he was free to say nothing, but there was a certain finesse to be observed in such matters, and a crude 'no' was not at all the thing. He was able to establish at least that this was the first time Wallington had visited Linton House.

On the way up to the Hall he said to Sylvia that her cousin seemed a dour fellow.

'Alf?' Bertie winced at the abbreviation. 'He's all right when you get to know him.'

'He said he was often in the south. What's his particular sphere of interest?'

'I don't know, I believe he's got some sort of export business around Durban. By the way, Bertie, how did you know Jimmy was away?'

'I saw him waving goodbye to you.' It would hardly do to say that he had been peeping through the curtains.

'Did you now? I was in bed when he went. You're a bit of a fibber, I'm afraid, Bertie.'

'Oh, I can't remember *how* I knew.' Really, it was too much to be taken up on every little point.

When they drove into the great courtyard and Sylvia got out of the car, however, he reflected that she looked very slenderly elegant, and that he was pleased to be with her. Bertie liked pretty women and they were safe with him, although he would not have thought of it that way.

He might have said, rather, that he would never have compromised a lady, with the implication that all sorts of things might be said and done providing that they stayed within the limits of discretion. It occurred to him that Sylvia was hardly staying within those limits when she allowed herself to be alone at Linton House with her South African cousin. Call me old-fashioned, Bertie said to himself, but I don't like it.

The Hall was a nineteenth-century manor house and by no means, as Bertie had often said, an architectural gem, but the lawns at the back where tea was served were undoubtedly fine. Sir Reginald Hussey was a building contractor who had been knighted for some dubious service to the export drive. He was in demand for opening fêtes and fund-raising enterprises, and the Husseys entertained a selection of local people to parties of one kind or another half-a-dozen times a year. The parties were always done in style, and this afternoon there were maids in white caps and aprons, and a kind of major-domo who wore a frock coat and white gloves. Sir Reginald was not in evidence, but Lady Hussey presided in a regal manner.

Of course Bertie knew that it was all ridiculously vulgar and ostentatious, but still he enjoyed himself. He kissed Lady Hussey's hand and said that the scene was quite entrancing, like a Victorian period picture, and he had an interesting chat with Lucy Broadhinton, who was the widow of an Admiral. Lucy was the president and Bertie the secretary of the local historical society, and they were great friends. She told him now in the strictest secrecy about the outrageous affair Mrs Monro was having with somebody who must be nameless, although from the details given Bertie was quite able to guess his identity. There were other titbits too, like the story of the scandalous misuse of the Church Fund restoration money. It was an enjoyable afternoon, and he fairly chortled about it on the way home.

'They're such snobby affairs,' Sylvia said. 'I don't know why I went.'

'You seemed to be having a good time. I was quite jealous.'

Sylvia had been at the centre of a very animated circle

of three or four young men. Her laughter at their jokes had positively rung out across the lawns, and Bertie had seen Lady Hussey give more than one disapproving glance in the direction of the little group. There was something undeniably attractive about Sylvia's gaiety and about the way in which she threw back her head when laughing, but her activities had a recklessness about them which was not proper for a lady. He tried to convey something of this as he drove back, but was not sure that she understood what he meant. He also broached delicately the impropriety of her being alone in the house with her cousin by asking when Jimmy would be coming back. In a day or two, she said casually. He refused her invitation to come in for a drink. He had no particular wish to see Alf Wallington again.

On the following night at about midnight, when Bertie was in bed reading, he heard a car draw up next door. Doors were closed, there was the sound of voices. Just to confirm that Jimmy was back, Bertie got out of bed and lifted an edge of the curtain. A man and a woman were coming out of the garage. The woman was Sylvia. The man had his arm round her, and as Bertie watched bent down and kissed her neck. Then they moved towards the front door, and the man laughed and said something. From his general build he might, seen in the dim light, have been Jimmy, but the voice had the distinctive South African accent of Wallington.

Bertie drew away from the window as though he had been scalded.

It was a feeling of moral responsibility that took him round to Linton House on the following day. To his surprise Jimmy Purchase opened the door.

'I – ah – though you were away.'

'Got back last night. What can I do for you?'

Bertie said that he would like to borrow the electric hedge-clippers, which he knew were in the garden shed. Jimmy led the way there and handed them over. Bertie said that he had heard the car coming back at about midnight.

'Yeah.' Jimmy had a deplorably Cockney voice, not at all out of the top drawer. 'That was Sylvia and Alf. He took her to a dance over at Ladersham. I was too fagged out, just wanted to get my head down.'

'Her cousin from South Africa?'

'Yeah, right, from the Cape. He's staying here for a bit. Plenty of room.'

Was he from the Cape or from Durban? Bertie did not fail to notice the discrepancy.

Bertie's bump of curiosity was even stronger than his sense of propriety. It became important, even vital, that he should know just what was going on next door. When he returned the hedge-cutters he asked them all to dinner, together with Lucy Broadhinton to make up the number. He took pains in preparing a delicious cold meal. The salmon was cooked to perfection, and the hollandaise sauce had just the right hint of something tart beneath its blandness.

The evening was not a success. Lucy had a long dress and Bertie wore a very smart velvet jacket, but Sylvia was dressed in sky-blue trousers and a vivid shirt, and the two men wore open-necked shirts and had a distinctly unkempt appearance. They had obviously been drinking before they arrived. Wallington tossed town Bertie's expensive hock as though it were water, and then said that South African wine had more flavour than that German stuff.

'You're from Durban, I believe, Mr Wallington.' Lucy fixed him with her Admiral's lady glance. 'My husband and I were there in the sixties, and thought it delightful. Do you happen to know the Morrows or the Page-Manleys? Mary Page-Manley gave such delightful parties.'

Wallington looked at her from under heavy brows. 'Don't know them.'

'You have an export business in Durban?'

'That's right.'

There was an awkward pause. Then Sylvia said, 'Alf's trying to persuade us to pay him a visit out there.'

'I'd like you to come out. Don't mind about him.' Wallington jerked his thumb at Jimmy. 'Believe me, we'd have a good time.'

'I do believe you, Alf.' She gave her head-back laugh,

showing the fine column of her neck. 'It's something we've forgotten here, how to have a good time.'

Jimmy Purchase had been silent during dinner. Now he said, 'People here just don't have the money. Like the song says, it's money makes the world go round.'

'The trouble in Britain is that too much money has got into the wrong hands.' Lucy looked round the table. Nobody seemed inclined to argue the point. 'There are too many grubby little people with sticky fingers.'

'I wish some of the green stuff would stick to my fingers,' Jimmy said, and hiccuped. Bertie realised with horror that he was drunk. 'We're broke, Sylvie, old girl.'

'Oh, shut up.'

'You don't believe me?' And he actually began to empty out his pockets. What appalling creatures the two men were, each as bad as the other. Bertie longed for the evening to end, and was delighted when Lucy rose to make a stately departure. He whispered an apology in the hall, but she told him not to be foolish, it had been fascinating.

When he returned Wallington said, 'What an old battleaxe. *Did you happen to know the Page-Manleys*. Didn't know they were still around, people like that.'

Sylvia was looking at Bertie. 'Alf, you're shocking our host.'

'Sorry, man, but honest, I thought they kept her sort in museums. Stuffed.'

'You mustn't say stuffed. That'll shock Bertie too.'

Bertie said stiffly, 'I am not in the least shocked, but I certainly regard it as the height of bad manners to criticise a guest in such a manner. Lucy is a very dear friend of mine.'

Sylvia at least had some understanding of his feelings. She said sorry and smiled, so that he was at once inclined to forgive her. Then she said it was time she took her rough diamonds home.

'Thanks for the grub,' Wallington said. Then he leaned across the dining table and shouted, 'Wake up, man, it's tomorrow morning already.' Jimmy had fallen asleep in his chair. He was hauled to his feet and supported across the garden.

Bertie called up Lucy the next morning and apologised

again. She said that he should think no more about it. 'I didn't take to that South African feller, though. Shouldn't be surprised if he turns out to be a bad hat. And I didn't care too much for your neighbours, if you don't mind my being frank.'

Bertie said of course not, although he reflected that there seemed to be a sudden spasm of frankness among his acquaintances. Mrs Purchase, Lucy said, had a roving eye. She left it at that, and they went on to discuss the agenda for the next meeting of the historical society.

Later in the morning there was a knock on the door. Jimmy was there, hollow-eyed and slightly green. ''Fraid we rather blotted out copybook last night. Truth is, Alf and I were fairly well loaded before we came round. Can't remember too much about it, but Syl said apologies were in order.'

Bertie asked when Sylvia's cousin was leaving. Jimmy Purchase shrugged and said he didn't know. Bertie nearly said that he ought not to leave the man alone with Sylvia, but refrained. He might be inquisitive, but he was also discreet.

A couple of nights later her was doing some weeding in the garden when he heard voices raised in Linton House. One was Jimmy's, the other belonged to Sylvia. They were in the sitting-room shouting at each other, not quite loudly enough for the words to be distinguishable. It was maddening not to know what was being said. Bertie moved along the fence separating the gardens, until he was as near as he could get without being seen. He was now able to hear a few phrases.

'Absolutely sick of it . . . drink because it takes my mind off . . . told you we have to wait . . .' That was Jimmy. Then Sylvia's voice, shrill as he had never heard it, shrill and sneering.

'Tell me the old old story . . . how long do we bloody well wait then . . . you said it would be finished by now.' An indistinguishable murmur from Jimmy. 'None of your business,' she said. More murmuring. 'None of your business what I do.' Murmur murmur. 'You said yourself we're broke.' To this there was some reply. Then she said clearly, 'I shall do what I like.'

'All right,' Jimmy said, so loudly that Bertie fairly jumped. There followed a sharp crack, which sounded like hand on flesh.

Sylvia said, 'You bastard, that's it, then.'

Nothing more. No sound, no speech. Bertie waited five minutes and then tiptoed away, fearful of being seen. Once indoors again he felt quite shaky, and had to restore himself by a nip of brandy. What had the conversation meant? Much of it was plain enough. Sylvia was saying that it was none of her husband's business if she carried on an affair. But what was it they had to wait for, what was it that should have been finished? A deal connected with the odious Alf? And where was Alf, who as Bertie had noticed went out into the village very little?

He slept badly, and was wakened in the middle of the night by a piercing, awful scream. He sat up in bed quivering, but the sound was not repeated. He decided that he must have been dreaming.

On the following day the car was not in the garage. Had Jimmy gone off again? He met Sylvia out shopping in the village, and she said that he had been called to an assignment at short notice.

'What sort of assignment?' He had asked before for the name of the paper Jimmy worked on, to be told that he was a freelance.

'A Canadian magazine. He's up in the Midlands, may be away a few days.'

Should he say something about the row? But that would have been indiscreet, and in any case Sylvia had such a wild look in her eye that he did not care to ask further questions. It was on that morning that he read about the Small Bank Robbers.

The Small Bank Robbers had been news for some months. They specialised in fast well-organised raids on banks, and had carried out nearly twenty of these in the past year. Several men were involved in each raid. They were armed, and did not hesitate to use coshes or revolvers when necessary. In one bank a screaming woman customer had suffered a fractured skull when hit over the head, and in another a guard who resisted the robbers had been shot and killed. The diminutive applied to them referred to the banks they robbed, not to their own physical dimensions. A bank clerk who had admitted giving information to the gang had asked why they were interested in his small branch bank, and had been told that they always raided small banks because they were much more vulnerable than large ones. After the arrest of this clerk the robbers seemed to have gone to ground. There had been no news of them for the last three or four weeks.

Bertie had heard about the Small Bank Robbers, but took no particular interest in them. He was a nervous man, and did not care for reading about crime. On this morning, however, his eye was caught by the heading: 'Small Bank Robbers. The South African Connection.' The story was a feature by the paper's crime reporter, Derek Holmes. He said that Scotland Yard knew the identities of some of the robbers, and described his own investigations, which led to the conclusion that three or four of them were in Spain. The article continued:

> But there is another connection, and a sinister one. The men in Spain are small fry. My researches suggest that the heavy men who organised the robberies, and were very ready to use violence, came from South Africa. They provided the funds and the muscle. Several witnesses who heard the men talking to each other or giving orders during the raids have said that they used odd accents. This has been attributed to the sound distortion caused by the stocking masks they wore, but two men I spoke to, both of whom have spent time in South Africa, said that they had *no doubt the accent was South African*.

The writer suggested that these men were now probably back in South Africa. But supposing that one of them was still in England, that he knew Jimmy and Sylvia and had a hold over them? Supposing, even, that they were minor members of the gang themselves? The thought made Bertie shiver with fright and excitement. What should or could he do about it? And where had Jimmy Purchase gone?'

Again he slept badly, and when he did fall into a doze it was a short one. He woke to find Wallington knocking on the door. Once inside the house he drew out a huge wad of notes, said that there was enough for everybody, and counted out bundles which he put on the table between them with a small decisive *thwack*. A second bundle, *thwack*, and a third, *thwack*. How many more? He tried to cry out, to protest, but the bundles went on, *thwack*, *thwack*, *thwack* . . .

He sat up in bed, crying out something inaudible. The thin grey light of early morning came through the curtains. There was a sound in the garden outside, a sound regularly repeated, the *thwack* of his dream. It took him in his slightly dazed state a little while to realise that if he went to the window he might see what was causing the sound. He tiptoed across the room and raised the curtain. He was trembling.

It was still almost dark, and whatever was happening was taking place at the back of Linton House, so that he could not see it. But as he listened to the regularly repeated sound, he had no doubt of its nature. Somebody was digging out there. The sound of the spade digging earth had entered his dream, and there was an occasional clink when it struck a stone. Why would somebody be digging at this time in the morning? He remembered that terrible cry on the previous night, the cry he had thought to be a dream. Supposing it had been real, who had cried out?

The digging stopped and two people spoke, although he could not hear the words or even the tones. One, light and high in pitch, was no doubt Sylvia, but was the other voice Wallington's? And if it was, had Jimmy Purchase gone away at all? In the half light a man and woman were briefly visible before they passed into the house. The man carried a spade, but his head was down and Bertie could not see his face, only his square bulky figure. He had little doubt that the man was Wallington.

That morning he went up to London. He had visited the city rarely since his retirement, finding that on each visit he was more worried and confused. The place seemed continually to change, so that what had been a landmark of some interest was now a kebab or hamburger restaurant. The article had appeared in the *Banner*, and their offices had moved from Fleet Street to somewhere off the Gray's Inn Road. He asked for Arnold Grayson, a deputy editor he had known slightly, to be told that Grayson had moved to another paper. He had to wait almost an hour before he was able to talk to Derek Holmes. The crime reporter remained staring at his desk while he listened to Bertie's story. During the telling of it he chewed gum and said 'Yup' occasionally.

'Yup,' he said again at the end. 'Okay, Mr Mays. Thanks.'

'What are you going to do about it?'

Holmes removed his gum and considered the question. 'Know how many people been in touch about that piece, saying they've seen the robbers, their landlord's one of them, they heard two South Africans talking in a bus about how the loot should be split, etcetera? One hundred and eleven. Half of 'em are sensationalists, the other half plain crazy.'

'But this is different.'

'They're all different. I shouldn'ta seen you only you mentioned Arnie, and he was a good friend. But what's it amount to? Husband and wife have a shindig, husband goes off, South African cousin's digging a flowerbed –'

'At that time in the morning?'

The reporter shrugged. 'People are funny.'

'Have you got pictures of the South Africans you say are involved in the robberies? If I could recognise Wallington – '

Holmes put another piece of gum in his mouth, chewed on it meditatively, and then produced half-a-dozen photographs. None of them resembled Wallington. Holmes shuffled the pictures together, put them away. 'That's it then.'

'But aren't you going to come down and look into it? I tell you I believe murder has been done. Wallington is her lover. Together they have killed Purchase.'

'If Wallington's lying low with his share of the loot, the last thing he'd do is get involved in this sort of caper. You know your trouble, Mr Mays? You've got an overheated imagination.'

If only he knew somebody at Scotland Yard! But there was no reason to think that they would take him any more seriously than the newspaper man had done. He returned feeling both chastened and frustrated. To his surprise Sylvia got out of another carriage on the train. She greeted him cheerfully.

'Hallo Bertie. I've just been seeing Alf off.'

'Seeing Alf off?' he echoed stupidly.

'Back to South Africa. He had a letter saying they needed him back there.'

'Back in Durban?'

'That's right.'

'Jimmy said he was from the Cape.'

'Did he? Jimmy often gets things wrong.'

It was not in Bertie's nature to be anything but gallant to a lady, even one he suspected of being a partner in murder. 'Now that you are a grass widow again, you must come in and have a dish of tea.'

'That would be lovely.'

'Tomorrow?'

'It's a date.'

They had reached his cottage. She pressed two fingers to her lips, touched his cheek with them. Inside the cottage the telephone was ringing. It was Holmes.

'Mr Mays? Thought you'd like to know. Your chum Purchase is just what he said, a freelance journalist. One or two of the boys knew him. Not too successful from what I hear.'

'So you did pay some attention to what I told you,' Bertie said triumphantly.

'Always try and check a story out. Nothing to this one, far as I can see.'

'Wallington has gone back to South Africa. Suddenly, just like that.'

'Has he now? Good luck to him.'

Triumph was succeeded by indignation. He put down the telephone without saying goodbye.

Was it all the product of an overheated imagination? He made scones for Sylvia's visit next day, and served them with his home-made blackcurrant conserve. Then he put the question that still worried him. He would have liked to introduce it delicately, but somehow didn't manage that.

'What was all that digging in the garden early the other morning?'

Sylvia looked startled, and then exclaimed as a fragment of the scone she was eating dropped on to her dress. When it had been removed she said, 'Sorry you were disturbed. It was Timmy.'

'Timmy?'

'Our tabby. He must have eaten something poisoned and he died. Poor Timmy. Alf dug a grave and we gave him a Christian burial.' With hardly a pause she went on, 'We're clearing out at the end of the week.'

'Leaving?' For a moment he could hardly believe it.

'Right. I'm a London girl at heart you know, always was. The idea of coming here was that Jimmy would be able to do some writing of his own, but that never seemed to work out, he was always being called away. If I'm in London I can get a job, earn some money. Very necessary at the moment. If Alf hadn't helped out, I don't know what we'd have done. It was a crazy idea coming down here, but then we're crazy people.'

And at the end of that week Sylvia went. Since the house had been rented furnished, she had only suitcases to take away. She came to say goodbye. There was no sign of Jimmy, and Bertie asked about him.

'Still up on that job. But anyway he wouldn't have wanted to come down and help, he hates things like that. Goodbye, Bertie, we'll meet again I expect.' A quick kiss on the cheek and she was driving off in her hired car.

She departed leaving all sorts of questions unanswered when Bertie came to think about it, mundane ones like an address if anybody should want to get in touch with her or with Jimmy, and things he would have liked to know, such as the reason for digging the cat's grave at such an extraordinary hour. He found himself more and more suspicious of the tale she had told. The row he had overhead could perhaps be explained by lack of money, but it seemed remarkable that Jimmy Purchase had not come back. Linton House was locked up and empty, but it was easy enough to get into the garden. The area dug up was just inside the boundary fence. It was difficult to see how much had been dug because there were patches of earth at either side, but it looked a large area to bury a cat.

On impulse one day, a week after Sylvia had gone, Bertie took a spade into the garden and began to dig. It proved to be quite hard work, and he went down two feet before reaching the body. It was that of a cat, one he vaguely remembered seeing in the house, but Sylvia's story of its death had been untrue. Its head was mangled, shattered by one or two heavy blows.

Bertie looked at the cat with distaste – he did not care for seeing dead things – returned it, and had just finished shovelling back the earth when he was hailed from the road. He turned, and with a sinking heart saw the local constable, PC Harris, standing beside his bicycle.

'Ah, it's you, Mr Mays. I was thinking it might be somebody with burglarious intent. Somebody maybe was going to dig a tunnel to get entrance into the house. But perhaps it was your *own* house you was locked out of.' PC Harris was well known as a local wag, and nobody laughed more loudly at his own jokes. He laughed heartily now. Bertie joined in feebly.

'But what *was* you doing digging in the next door garden may I ask?'

What could he say? I was digging for a man, but only found a cat? Desperately Bertie said, 'I'd – ah – lost something and thought it might have got in here. I was just turning the earth.'

The constable shook his head. 'You was trespassing, Mr Mays. This is not your property.'

'No, of course not. It won't happen again. I'd be glad if you could forget it.' He approached the constable, a pound note in his hand.

'No need for that, sir, which might be construed as a bribe and hence an offence in itself. I shall not be reporting the matter on this occasion, nor enquiring further into the whys and wherefores, but would strongly advise you in future to keep within the bounds of your own property.'

Pompous old fool, Bertie thought, but said that of course he would do just that. He scrambled back into his own garden, aware that he made a slightly ludicrous figure. PC Harris, in a stately manner, mounted his bicycle and rode away.

That was almost, but not quite, the end of the story. Linton House was empty for a few weeks and then let again, to a family called Hobson who had two noisy children. Bertie had as little to do with them as possible. He was very conscious of having been made to look a fool, and there was nothing he disliked more than that. He was also aware of a disinclination in himself to enter Linton house again.

In the late spring of the following year he went to Sardinia for a holiday, driving around on his own, looking at the curious nuraghi and the burial places made from gigantic blocks of stone which are called the tombs of the giants. He drove up the western coast in a leisurely way, spending long mornings and afternoons over lunches and dinners in the small towns, and then moving inland to bandit country. He was sitting nursing a drink in a square at Nuoro, which is the capital of the central province, when he heard his name called.

It was Sylvia, so brown that he hardly recognised her. 'Bertie, what are you doing here?'

He said that he was on holiday, and returned the question.

'Just come down to shop. We have a house up in the hills, you must come and see it. Darling, look who's here.'

A bronzed Jimmy Purchase approached across the square. Like Sylvia he seemed in fine spirits, and endorsed enthusiastically the suggestion that Bertie should come out to their house. It was a few miles from the city on the slopes of Mount Ortobene, a long low white modern house at the end of a rough track. They sat in a courtyard and ate grilled fish, with which they drank a hard dry local white wine. Bertie felt his natural curiosity rising. How could he ask questions without appearing to be – well – nosy? Over coffee he said that he supposed Jimmy was out here on an assignment.

It was Sylvia who answered. 'Oh no, he's given all that up since the book was published.'

'The book?'

'Show him, Jimmy.' Jimmy went into the house. He returned with a book which said on the cover *My Tempestuous Life*. As told by Anita Sorana to Jimmy Purchase.

'You've heard of her?'

It would have been difficult not to have heard of Anita Sorana. She was a screen actress famous equally for her temperament, her five well-publicised marriages, and the variety of her love affairs.

'It was fantastic luck when she agreed that Jimmy should write her autobiography. It was all very hush hush and we had to pretend that he was off on assignments when he was really with Anita.'

Jimmy took it up. 'Then she'd break appointments, say she wasn't in the mood to talk. A few days afterwards she'd ask to see me at a minute's notice. Then Sylvia started to play up—'

'I thought he was having an affair with her. She certainly fancied him. He swears he wasn't, but I don't know. Anyway, it was worth it.' She yawned.

'The book was a success?'

Jimmy grinned, teeth very white in his brown face. 'I'll say. Enough for me to shake off the dust of Fleet Street.'

So the quarrel was explained, and Jimmy's sudden absences, and his failure to return. After a glass of some fiery local liqueur Bertie felt soporific, conscious that he had drunk a little more than usual. There was some other question he wanted to ask, but he did not remember it until they were driving him down the mountain, back to his hotel in Nuoro.

'How is your cousin?'

Jimmy was driving. 'Cousin?'

'Mr Wallington, Sylvia's cousin from South Africa.'

Sylvia, from the back of the car, said, 'Alf's dead.'

'Dead!'

'In a car accident. Soon after he got back to South Africa. Wasn't it sad?'

Very few more words were spoken before they reached the hotel and said goodbye. The heat of the hotel room and the wine he had drunk made him fall asleep at once. After a couple of hours he woke, sweating, and wondered if he believed what he had been told. Was it possible to make enough money from 'ghosting' (he had heard that was the word) a life story to retire to Sardinia? It seemed unlikely. He lay on his back in the dark room, and it seemed to him that he saw with terrible clarity what had happened.

Wallington was one of the Small Bank Robbers, and he had come to the Purchases looking for a safe place to stay. He had his money, what Holmes had called the loot, with him, and they had decided to kill him for it. The quarrel had been about when Wallington would be killed, the sound that wakened him in the night had been Wallington's death cry. Jimmy had merely pretended to go away that night, and had returned to help Sylvia dispose of the body. Jimmy dug the grave and they put Wallington in it. Then the cat had been killed and put into a shallow grave on top of the body. It was the killing of the cat, those savage blows on its head, that somehow horrified Bertie most.

He cut short his holiday, took the next plane back. At home he walked round to the place where he had dug up the cat. The Hobsons had put in bedding plants, and the wallflowers were flourishing. He had read somewhere that flowers always flourished over a grave.

'Not thinking of trespassing again, I hope, Mr Mays?'

It was PC Harris, red-faced and jovial.

Bertie shook his head. What he had imagined in the hotel room might be true, but then again it might not. Supposing that he went to the police, supposing he was able to convince them that there was something in his story, supposing they dug up the flower bed and found nothing but the cat? He would be the laughing stock of the neighbourhood.

Bertie Mays knew that he would say nothing.

'I reckon you was feeling a little bit eccentric that night you was doing the digging,' PC Harris said sagely.

'Yes, I think I must have been.'

'They make a fine show, them wallflowers. Makes you more cheerful, seeing spring flowers.'

'Yes,' said Bertie Mays meekly. 'They make a fine show.'

VAMPIRE

Hilary Norman

Do you believe in vampires? Probably not. Neither did I until I met William and then, along with everything else in my frame of reference, that changed . . .

We met ten years ago at a wine and cheese party – the splendid kind where the Bries overflow ripely, the Stiltons crumble, and the wines are never plonk.

I remember I came manless to the throng: something I greatly loved doing, gregarious and youthful as I was then. There was always someone to talk to – I didn't care if they were male or female, I just enjoyed people. And so it was the second I clapped eyes on William Caulard; I enjoyed him.

He was at the buffet, a bottle of claret in his hand, and it was his fingers I noticed first. They were beautiful; tapering and white. And then I saw his eyes. They were gazing into the wine; the darkest, blackest eyes I'd ever seen.

I remember feeling intrusive, but I spoke anyway. 'Have you tasted it?'

I recall he drew his eyes from the dark liquid with what seemed like pain; but I remember, too, that when they refocused on me, the pain was dislodged and swam away and clear, frank pleasure took its place.

'Yes.' His deep, vibrant voice touched a nerve in my spine, making me quiver.

I saw that the bottle was still corked.

'I tasted it at its birth, before it was captured and imprisoned in this bottle.'

I read the label. '1961 . . . Was that a good year?'

He smiled, and his lips stretched generously and linked with his eyes. 'Quite good, yes,' he said, 'but I sampled the first drops of the first vintage.'

'But—'

'Yes,' he said softly. 'I am old – older than I look.'

It was true. He did not look old; he had the posture and leanness of a man of twenty-five. But I watched him and knew he was, as he said, old. Curiously, it did not trouble me at all.

'What is your name?' I asked.

He told me, and asked mine.

'Miranda.'

Again he smiled. 'Of course,' he said.

We left together, William Caulard and I, and went to Hampstead Heath, and though it had been cloudy and moist when we left the party, as soon as we set foot on the soft turf of the Heath the clouds parted and the moon, full and cool, guided us to the sweet-smelling copse where we sank to the ground and made love.

'Plighting our troth,' I remember I whispered, and then blushed. 'Shakespeare.'

'I know,' he said. 'I was in Stratford when he wrote the lines.'

'Are you a ghost?' I asked, wondering.

'No.' His lips, warm and firm, brushed my neck. 'But you, my Miranda, like Juliet, were a virgin.'

It was true. I had been pure and innocent, in spite of many previous boyfriends; but there I lay, stretched out on the damp grass, with my strange first love. 'If you're not a ghost, William Caulard, then what are you?'

'A man.'

I shook my head, and my long hair tangled with the nettles. 'Not just a man. Tell me, please.'

'A man,' he insisted. 'All else must wait.'

And so he made me his again, and before first light, William Caulard brought me to my door and asked me to become his wife.

'But I don't know you,' I murmured.

His eyes hypnotised me. 'You know me, Miranda my

love.' And again he brushed my neck with his mouth. 'Marry me.'

And I said yes.

He told me on our wedding night. 'I am a vampire,' he said in his beautiful voice. 'I have lived for four hundred and sixty-three years, and you are the first woman I have ever loved as a mere man.'

I believed him.

'Why didn't you tell me before?'

'Fear – that you might refuse me.'

'I couldn't have refused you.'

'No.'

We curled together then, and rolled and tumbled and agonised and climaxed. 'Do you want my blood?' I gasped, as my body arched.

He pulled away, his face angry. 'No!'

'Why not?'

'Because I love you.'

'But don't you need blood to live?'

'Quiet, Miranda!' he commanded. 'Later – later I will explain. Now let me lie with you quietly, as your husband, and drink your soul.'

What girl could resist that?

He did explain later. It was a fallacy, he said, that vampires required blood to live. He told me it was instead an inherited, or sometimes transmitted deep-rooted addiction – far harder to break than ordinary mortal addictions to nicotine, alcohol or other drugs.

I asked how he would survive without blood and he explained that it was more than the blood itself, it was the actual act of sucking at the throat. He said he intended to fight his own addiction with all his might. 'And if I fail, Miranda, it will not be with you.'

I remember rising from our marriage bed then naked and resolute. 'No!'

'What?'

'Never with anyone else. You have a wife now; you must abide by your vows. If you falter, it must be with me.'

'But it would weaken – even endanger you.'

'Better your wife than an innocent stranger.'

He gave me his hand, and his eyes were full of love. 'So be it. Vampires never lie.'

And so began the long, hard period of William's withdrawal from his addiction of more than four centuries. Only his great love for me, I believe, made it possible; but I was tortured seeing what he endured.

For a time he grew weak, and once – after he had explained that his blood level was now precariously low – I brought him bull's blood from the butcher; but he grew angry and smashed the jar, and I understood that I was cruel to tempt him.

But two years later, it was over. William was triumphant. He could endure week after week without thinking of his addiction, without yearning for the salty taste or the sensation of the submitting artery.

It was time, he said, for us to think of children. 'But can we?' I asked in some concern. 'Will they be . . .?'

'Human?' he said. 'I think so. I, after all, became a vampire by transference, not inheritance.'

I considered this in silence. 'And would they be . . . mortal?' I asked then, trembling because I contemplated my infants' death even before their conception.

'I have never impregnated a woman before. I cannot be sure.'

And so I stopped taking my small white pills and left the fate of my womb to God and William.

All our three children appear perfectly normal. Michael, the oldest, displays no signs of inheriting more from William than black eyes and a deep temperament. Lucy is golden, a cheeky enchantress who holds her father in her plump palm, and Sam, the baby, is a spiky little soul with a mind of his own.

It was having Sam that began our crisis – Sam, and William's work.

Haven't I mentioned his work? Yes, of course he works – how else could we manage? Ah, you're worried about daylight. You think all vampires crumble into dust when struck by the sun. Another fallacy.

In truth, William does not like the sun, because the skin of a vampire is easily burned. If we were to spend long periods in bright sunshine, he might become quite ill. But it's no worse than that and, in any case, William says he has grown less sensitive because of his blood-free diet.

Anyway, his work: William is a fashion designer. Haven't you heard of Caulard? It was he who caused such a stir a few years ago when he designed those outrageously-priced evening dresses with sixteenth-century ruffs.

Anyway, our crisis: it was mostly my fault. Three lovely children, a comfortable house, an attractive unique husband . . . a woman risks becoming placid. I became smug. And what inevitably happens when a wife stumbles into complacency? Her husband strays.

It was also Cassandra's fault – one of the Caulard models. She was five feet eleven inches of high-breasted, velvet-skinned, doe-eyed youth . . . with lovely veins – William's downfall. And mine.

I didn't just get smug, I got round. I didn't bother as much with exercises after Sam as with the other two.

I'd also gone off sex. For the first time since Hampstead Heath, I didn't like William touching me. And it's one thing for a man like William Caulard to swear off blood, but quite another to abandon his natural human desires too.

And there was Cassandra, at work with her slender neck and young breasts and perfect veins. 'I'm working late again tonight,' he'd telephone from the office.

'Fine,' I'd say stiffly. 'I'll be asleep when you get home.'

How could he? It wasn't just the affair I minded – though, of course, I *did* mind – it was what he might be doing to Cassandra that terrified me.

But how could I stop it? I dieted, of course, and bought new nightdresses and a pair of skinny jeans with a sexy motif on the behind, which I threw in the dustbin when I got home – mutton dressed as lamb. There was no way I could compete with Cassandra, so why bother to try?

It was the accident, in the end, that gave me back my husband.

The phone rang one Tuesday morning at eleven. 'Mrs Caulard?'

'Yes.' It was Lucy's headmistress calling. Her voice

sounded soft and anxious. 'I'm afraid I have to tell you there's been an accident.'

'Lucy?' I whispered stupidly.

She was in the hospital by the time I saw her, lying on a trolley in Casualty, covered with a red blanket. Apart from the slight fluttering of her lashes, she might have been dead.

'She needs a transfusion,' a doctor said.

'Of course,' I said, ready to sign consent.

'The trouble is she's a very rare blood group . . . Do you know your blood type, Mrs Caulard?'

Ice-cold, I nodded. 'O.' I was no good to them, it was William's blood that filled Lucy's veins.

Soon, his eyes blacker than ever with fear, he was beside me. 'What happened?'

I gulped. 'She ran out of the playground into the road. No one knows why. They took her away. She needs a transfusion.'

'Oh my God!'

I looked at him. 'And she has your rare blood group,' I said. 'They're trying to match it now.'

He jumped up, seeking anyone who would tell him where to go to give his daughter his blood.

I pulled at his sleeve. 'William, sit down.'

He was trembling.

'It would be dangerous for you to give blood, wouldn't it? Isn't your level low already?'

His eyes were angry. 'Who's more important, Lucy or me?'

'I don't know,' I said.

I think that was the moment when the hole in our marriage was mended – the instant when I saw I might lose him for ever, and he saw how much I loved him. He offered me his arm, and I leaned against him. 'What about Cassandra?'

He stiffened. I don't think he realised I knew. 'It's over.'

'Since when?' I asked.

'Now.' At least he was honest.

He sat forward. 'Where is everyone, for God's sake?'

I squeezed his hand. 'They said she's stable. I think they're contacting other hospitals.'
'What for?'
'To find the right blood.'
'But *I* have the right blood.'
'Yes, but they'd rather take it from a bottle than your veins.'
'Why?' he asked sharply. 'What did you tell them?'
'I said you're a haemophiliac,' I answered quietly. 'After all, I could hardly tell them the truth about you, could I?'
'What if they don't find any?'
'Then we'll say I was lying, and you can give yours.'
He turned my face to his, and his eyes were tender and savage at the same time.
They found Lucy's blood type at the Blood Donor Centre in Hammersmith, and our little girl was right as rain two weeks after.
So were we.
I expect you're still worried about Cassandra. That night, after they told us Lucy would be all right, I asked him: 'William, did you . . .?'
'What?'
'With Cassandra – you know.'
A look of surprise crossed his face, as if he'd thought me wiser. 'It isn't important now, Miranda.'
'Not *important*?' I echoed incredulously.
'No. These things happen. She's not important to me.'
'But what might happen is important, surely. What about the others?' I lowered my voice. 'Is Cassandra a vampire now?'
His eyes creased, and he began to laugh.
'William!'
'Oh, Miranda!'
'I see nothing to laugh at. I told you when we married that I wouldn't stand for that. I said if you weakened, it must be with me and no one else.'
'Yes,' he said, still rocking with laughter.
'Well?' I demanded indignantly. 'I see nothing funny about starting a vampire colony in London!'
'Oh, darling Miranda,' he chortled, and took me in his arms. 'I thought you meant had I slept with Cassandra,

and of course, you know we had, and I am sorry, but it meant nothing. How could you possibly imagine I would betray you any other way?'

'It was her veins,' I muttered, blushing darkly.

He spluttered more wildly than ever, and his behaviour was so uncharacteristic of the William Caulard I had been married to for so long, that for the very first time I found myself wondering if perhaps he'd been less than truthful these past ten years, and if, maybe, he was not four hundred and thirty years older than me, after all.

My eyes grew huge.

'William Caulard,' I demanded indignantly, 'have you been lying to me all these years? Because if you have, I think I'll kill you before I divorce you!'

A look of purest innocence passed over his face, and he said, in his most beautiful voice, still the colour of antique claret: 'No, Miranda, I haven't. Surely you remember what I told you – that vampires never lie.'

I'm still not altogether sure if I believe him.

PAPERWORK

Ruth Rendell

My earliest memories are of paper. I can see my grandmother sitting at the table she used for a desk, a dining-table made to seat twelve, with her scrapbook before her and the scissors in her hand. She called it her research. For years three newspapers came into that house every day and each week half a dozen magazines. Her post was large and she wrote at least one letter each day. My grandfather was a solicitor in our nearest town, four miles away, and he brought work home, paperwork. He always carried two briefcases and they were full of documents.

Because he was a man he had a study of his own and a proper desk. The house was quite large enough for my grandmother to have had a study too, but that was not a word she would have used in connection with herself. Her table was in the sewing room, though no sewing was ever done in it in my time. She spent most of her day in there, covering reams of paper with her small handwriting or pasting cuttings into a succession of scrapbooks. Sometimes she cut things out of books and one of the small miseries of living in that house was to open a book in the library and find part of a chapter missing or the one poem you wanted gone from an anthology.

The sewing room door was always left open. This was so that my grandmother might hear what was going on in the rest of the house, not to indicate that visitors would be welcome. She would hear me coming up the stairs, no matter how careful I was to tread silently, and call out before I reached the open door, 'No children in here, please,' as if it were a school or a big family of sisters and brothers living there instead of just me.

It was a very large house, though not large enough or handsome enough to be a stately home. If visitors go there now in busloads, as I have heard they do, it is not for architecture or antiquity, but for another, uglier, reason. Eighteen fifty-one was the year of its building and the principal material used was white bricks which are not really white but the pale glabrous grey of cement. The windows were just too wide for their height, the front door too low for the fat pillars which flanked it and the portico they supported, a plaster dome shaped like the crown of my grandfather's bowler hat and which put me in mind, when I was older, of a tomb in one of London's bigger cemeteries. Or rather, when I saw such a tomb, I would be reminded of my grandparents' house.

It was a long way from the village. The town, as I have said, was four miles away, and anything bigger, anywhere in which life and excitement might be going on, three times that distance. There were no buses. If you wanted to go out you went by car and if there was no car you walked. My grandfather, wearing his bowler, drove himself and his briefcases to work in a black Daimler. Sometimes I used to wonder how my mother had gone, when I was a baby and she left me with her parents, by what means she had made her escape. It was not my grandmother but the daily woman, Mrs Poulter, who told me my mother had no car of her own.

'She couldn't drive, pet. She was too young to learn, you see. You're too young to drive when you're sixteen but you're not too young to have a baby. Funny, isn't it?'

Perhaps someone had called for her. Anyway, a denizen of that house would be used to walking. Had she gone in daylight or after dark? Had she discussed her departure with her parents, asked their permission to go perhaps, or had she done what Mrs Poulter called a moonlight flit? Sometimes I imagined her writing a note and fastening it to her pillow with the point of a knife. I used to wonder about these things, for I had plenty of time and solitude for wondering. One day I overhead my grandmother say to an acquaintance from the village, 'I have never allowed myself to get fond of the child, purely as a matter of self-preservation. Suppose its mother decides to come back for it? She is its mother. She would have a right to it. And then where would I be? If I allowed myself to get fond of it, I mean?'

That was when I was about seven. A person of seven is too old to be referred to as 'it'. Perhaps a person of seven months or even seven days would be too old. But overhearing this did not upset me. It cheered me up and gave me hope. My mother would come for me. At least there was a strong possibility she would come, enough to keep my grandmother from loving me. And I understood somehow that she was tempted to love me. The temptation was there and she had to prevent herself from yielding to it, so that she was in a very different position from my grandfather who, I am sure, had no temptation to resist.

It was at about this time that I took it into my head that the scrapbook my grandmother was currently working on was concerned with my mother. The newspaper cuttings and the magazine photographs were of her. She might be an actress or a model or some other kind of famous person. Did my grandparents get letters from her? It was my job or Evie's to take up the post and on my way to the dining room where my grandparents always had a formal breakfast together, I would examine envelopes. Most were typewritten. All the letters that came for my grandfather were typed letters in envelopes with a typed address. But regularly there came to my grandmother, every two or three weeks, a letter in a blue envelope with a London postmark and the address in a handwriting not much more formed than my own, the capitals disproportionately large and the g's and y's with long tails that curled round like the Basenji's. I was sure these letters were from my mother and that some of them, much cut about, found their way into the scrapbook.

If children are not loved, they say, when they are little, they never learn to love. I am grateful therefore that there was one person in that house to love me and a creature whom I could love. My grandparents, you understand, were not old. My mother was sixteen when I was born, so they were still in their early forties. Of course they seemed old to me, though not old as Evie was. Even then I could appreciate that Evie belonged in quite a different generation, the age group of my schoolfellows' grandmothers.

She was some sort of relation. She may even have been my grandmother's aunt. I believe she had lived with them since they were first married as a kind of housekeeper, running things and organising things and doing the cooking. It was her home but she was there on sufferance and she was frightened of my grandmother. When I wanted information I went to Mrs Poulter, who was not afraid of what she said because she did not care if she got the sack.

'They need me more than I need them, pet. There's a dozen houses round here where they'd fall over themselves to get me.'

The trouble was that she knew very little. She had come to work there after my mother left and what she knew was from hearsay and gossip. Her name she knew, and her age of course, and that she wanted to marry my father, though my grandparents would have liked her to marry anyone but him.

'They called her Sandy. I expect it was because she had ginger hair.'

'Was it the same colour as the Basenji?' I said, but Mrs Poulter could not tell me that. She had never seen my mother.

Evie was afraid to answer my questions. I promised faithfully I would say nothing to my grandmother of what she told me but she distrusted me and I daresay she was right. But it was very tantalising because what there was to know Evie knew. She knew everything, as much as my grandparents did. She even knew who the letters were from but she would never say. My grandmother was capable of throwing her out.

'She wanted to throw your mother out,' said Mrs Poulter. 'Before you were born, I mean. I suppose I shouldn't be telling you this at your age but you've got to know some time. It was Evie stopped her. Well, that's what they say. Though how she did it when she never stands up for herself I wouldn't know.'

Basenjis are barkless dogs. They can learn to bark if

they are kept with other sorts of dogs but left to themselves they never do, though they squeak a bit and make grunting sounds. Basenjis are clean and gentle and it is a libel to say they are bad-tempered. They are an ancient breed of hound dog native to Central Africa, where they are used to point and retrieve and drive quarry into a net. Since I left that house I have always had a Basenji of my own and now I have two. What could be more natural than that I should love above all other objects of affection the kind I first loved?

My grandparents were not fond of animals and Evie was allowed to keep the Basenji only because he was a barkless dog. I am sure my grandmother put him through a barking test before she admitted him to the house. Evie and the Basenji had a whole section of it to live in by themselves. If this sounds like uncharacteristic generosity on my grandmother's part, in fact their rooms were two north-facing attics, the backstairs and what Mrs Poulter called the old scullery. All the time I was not at school (taken there and fetched by Evie in the Morris Minor Estate car) I spent with her and the Basenji in the old scullery. And in the summer, when the evenings were light, I took the Basenji for his walks.

You will have been wondering why I made no attempt to examine those scrapbooks or read those letters. Why did I never go into the sewing room in my grandmother's absence or penetrate my grandfather's study in the daytime? I tried. Though my grandmother seldom went out, she seemed to me to have an almost supernatural ability to be in two places, or more than two places, at once. She was a very tall thin woman with a long narrow face and dark flat rather oily hair which looked as if it were painted on rather than grew. I swear I have stood at the top of the first flight of stairs and seen her at her table, the scissors in her hand, her head turned as she heard the sound of my breathing, have run down and caught her just inside the drawing room door, one long dark bony hand on the brass knob, twisted away swiftly and glimpsed her in the library, taking from the shelves a book destined for mutilation.

It was all my fancy, no doubt. But she was ever-alert,

keeping watch. For what? To prevent my discovery of her secrets? She was a mistress of the art of secrecy. She loved it for its own sake. At mealtimes she locked the sewing room door. Perhaps she hung the key around her neck. Certainly she always wore a long chain, though what was on the end of it I never saw, for it was tucked into the vee of her dark dress. The study was never locked up but all the papers inside it were. One day, from the doorway, I saw the safe. I saw my grandfather take down the painting of an old man in a wig and a red coat and move this way and that a dial in the wall behind it.

On Fridays Evie put all the week's newspapers out for the dustmen, a sizeable pile which I went through in the hope of finding clues. Windows had been cut out of most of them, sometimes from the sports pages, sometimes from the arts section, from the home news and the foreign news. Once, in possession of a mutilated copy of *The Times*, I managed by wheedling and importunity to persuade Mrs Poulter to bring me an identical undamaged copy which she helped herself to from another house where she cleaned. But the cut-out pieces had been only a report of a tennis tournament and a photograph of a new kind of camellia exhibited at the Chelsea Flower Show.

I used to badger Evie about my mother but she would never answer. She told me frankly that she dared not answer. But at last, driven mad by my pestering, she must have said something to my grandmother, for one morning at the breakfast table after my grandfather had left, after I had brought in the post which included one of the letters in the blue envelopes, my grandmother turned to face me.

'These letters which you have been so curious about come from someone I was at school with. Her writing is rather immature, isn't it?'

I blushed. I said quite feverishly. 'Tell me about my mother.'

The tone didn't change or the look. 'Her name is Alexandra. I seldom hearing anything of her. I believe she has married.'

'Why didn't she have me adopted?' I said. 'Why didn't you?'

'Naturally I can't answer for her. I would have had

you adopted if it had been in my power. The mother's consent is needed in these matters.'

'Why didn't she want me? Why did she go away?'

'I shan't answer any more questions,' my grandmother said. 'You'll know one day. When we're dead you'll know. All about your mother and what little is known of your father, about the murder, if it was murder, and everything else. And you can tell Evie from me that if she gives you any information about what is no business whatsoever of hers I shan't see it my duty to give her or that dog of hers houseroom any longer.'

I passed this message on to Evie. What else could I do? My grandmother always meant what she said, she was a fearful woman, a cold force to be reckoned with. But the murder – what was the murder? In the ten years before I was born there had been two in the part of the country where we lived. A woman had killed her husband and then herself. A young man, not a local, had been found dead at the wheel of his car which was parked at the edge of a wood. He had been shot through the head. They never found who did it. During my childhood – I was in my teens by then – a local man was found hanged, had hanged himself I suppose, because he was about to be arrested for fraud. There were hints of an unknown partner in this swindle. I didn't have to ask Mrs Poulter about these things, they were common knowledge, but I did ask her what they had to do with us.

'They weren't even near here, pet,' she said. 'The woman who killed her husband and gassed herself, she'd only been living in her house for six months. And that young fellow, he drove up here from London, he was a stranger.'

She was more easily able to explain what my grandmother meant when she said I would know everything one day, when they were dead.

'They're going to leave you this house and its contents. I know it for a fact. He got me in there to be a witness to their wills.'

'But they don't even like me,' I said.

'You're their flesh and blood. They like you as much as they like anyone, pet. Anyway it's no big deal, is it? Who'd want it? Great white elephant, it's not worth much.'

Not then, perhaps, not then.

When I was fifteen and the Basenji was twelve and Evie getting on for eighty, my grandfather went out into the wood with his gun one morning and shot himself. They said it was an accident. After the funeral my grandmother got a carpenter in from London and had him build her three cupboards in the sewing room. She had the kind of doors put on them which security firms recommend nowadays for the front doors of London flats. Into these cupboards she placed the contents of my grandfather's wall safe and all his documents. She probably put her own complete scrapbooks in there too, for I never saw her at work with scissors and paste again and there was no more mutilation of books.

There were rumours, and more than rumours, that my grandfather had been in trouble. Converting his clients' money to his own use or persuading elderly women to make wills in his favour – something of that sort. I suppose that when he went out into the wood that morning it was because he was afraid of criminal proceedings. His death must have averted that. His secrets were in the papers my grandmother hid away. She changed after he was dead, becoming even more cold and remote, and the few acquaintances she had she shunned. It was a cold house, though she had never seemed to feel ill. She did then. Evie began lighting a fire in the grate and for some reason unknown to me it was my grandfather's cigarette lighter she used to light it, a silver object in the shape of an Aladdin lamp which stood in the centre of the mantel piece. For a while my grandmother continued to leave the sewing room door open and when I passed and looked in the fire would be alight and she would be writing. She was always writing. Memoirs? A diary? A novel?

Records of births, marriages and deaths were kept at Somerset House then. When I reached the age my mother was when I was born I went by train to London and looked her up in the appropriate great tomes. Alexandra was her name, as my grandmother had said (she never told lies) and she had married, as she also said, a man called Jeremy Harper-Green. They had two children, the Harper-Greens, a boy of six and a girl of four. I think it was when I saw this that I understood I would never meet my mother now.

The Basenji was the first to die. He was fifteen and he had had a good life. Evie and I buried him at the bottom of the garden which was on the side of a hill and from which you could look across the beautiful countryside of Derbyshire and see in the distance the landscape Capability Brown made at Chatsworth. It was winter, the woods dark and the hillsides covered in snow. I dug the grave but Evie was there with me in the biting wind. She caught a cold which turned to pneumonia and a week later she was dead too.

There was nothing to keep me after that. I packed up everything I owned into two suitcases and went to the sewing room and knocked on the door. For the past year she had kept that door closed. She said, 'Who is it?' not 'Come in', though it could only have been me or a ghost.

I told her I was leaving, I was going to London. She asked no questions about money so I was spared telling her that I had taken all the notes I found hidden in Evie's rooms, in old handbags and stuffed into vases and wrapped in a scarf at the back of a drawer. Evie had told me often enough she wanted me to have what she left behind. My grandmother didn't ask me but she did me the one service I ever remember receiving from her hands. She gave me the name and address of that old school friend, the one who wrote the letters in the blue envelopes and who was part owner of a London employment agency.

After that she shook hands with me as if I were a caller who had dropped in for half an hour. She didn't get out of her chair. She shook her head in a rueful way and said, not to me but as if there were someone else standing in the doorway to hear her, 'Who would have thought it would have gone on for eighteen years?'

Then she picked up her pen and turned back to whatever it was she was writing.

That was nearly thirty years ago. The friend with the employment agency got me a job. I stayed with her until I found a room of my own. I have prospered. I am managing director of my own company now and if I am not rich I am comfortably off. My marriage lasted only a short time but there is nothing unusual in that. Children I never wanted and I have none. Five Basenjis have been my companions through the years and they have been more to me than lovers or children.

Mrs Poulter told me my grandmother had left me the house. The chance of this I believed I lost for ever on the day I left. I had never heard from my grandmother, had written no letters and received none. I seldom thought of her. Then one Monday morning three years ago a letter came from a law firm telling me she had died and left me the house. The funeral had taken place. I wondered who had seen to the arrangements. The Harper-Greens? If they expected a legacy they were disappointed, for it all came to me, the house and its contents, the grounds from which you could see the meadows and woods of Chatsworth.

Now I should know the answers to those questions, the solutions to many mysteries. I drove up there one morning in autumn, my pair of Basenjis with me in the back of the estate car. Was the truth that she had loved me all along, valued me in her cold inexpressive way? Or had she simply not bothered to change her will because, though she cared nothing for me, there was no one else she cared more for?

We let ourselves into the house, the dogs and I. It was dusty and the ceilings hung with cobwebs, but the smell that met me as I walked up the stairs was the smell of paper, old paper turned yellow with time and packed away in airless places. The sewing room door was not locked. There were ashes in the grate and the silver Aladdin's lamp lighter still on the mantelpiece. A sheet of paper lay on the blotter on the table that was big enough to seat twelve. There were lines of writing on it, the final sentence broken off, the fountain pen lying where my grandmother had dropped it and a splutter of ink trailing from the last, half-completed word.

With the keys from the bunch I held I unlocked the burglar-proof cupboard doors. It was all there, all the secrets, in fifty scrapbooks, in a thousand letters received and a thousand copies of letters sent, in a hundred diaries, in deeds and agreements and contracts, in unnumbered handwritten manuscripts. The smell of paper, or perhaps it was the smell of ink, was acrid and nauseating. The dogs padded about the room, sniffing in corners, sniffing along skirting boards and around chair legs, sniffing and holding up their heads as if in thought, as if considering what it was they had smelt.

I began emptying the cupboards. Everything would have to be examined page by page, word by word, and in this house, in this room. How could I take it away except in a removal van? I imagined the misery of it, as sad and dreadful things were slowly revealed. Presently I got up and took my grandfather's silver lighter off the mantelpiece. I struck it with my thumb and the flame flared orange and blue. The Basenjis were watching me. They watched me as I applied the lighter to the pile of paper and the flame began to lick across the first sheet, lick, die, smoulder, lick, crackle, burst into bright flame.

I picked up the dogs, one under each arm, and ran down the stairs. The front door slammed behind me. What happened to the keys I don't know, I think I left them inside. I didn't look back but drove fast away and back to London.

It had been insured but of course I didn't claim on the insurance. The land belongs to me and I could have another house built on it but I never shall. Two years ago a tour company wrote to me and asked if they might bring parties to look at the burnt-out shell as part of a scenic Derbyshire round trip. So now the coach that goes to Chatsworth and Haddon Hall and Bess of Hardwick's house, follows the winding road up the hill to my childhood home, shows off to tourists the blackened ruin and the incomparable view.

I will never forget the way the police told me my house had burned down. Later they hinted at arson and this is how the guide explains things to visitors. But that evening when I had only been back a few hours, the police came and spoke to me very gently and carefully. I must sit down, keep calm, prepare myself for something upsetting.

They called it bad news.

Postscript

Dear Reader,

If you have enjoyed reading this collection of stories, and if you liked them half as much as I did, then why not make a small personal donation direct to the National AIDS Trust? If you are able to do so, please accept my personal thanks on behalf of the Trust.

John Gielgud

Sir John Gielgud

To: National AIDS Trust,
6th Floor,
Eileen House,
80 Newington Causeway,
London SE1 6EF

☐ I have pleasure in enclosing my cheque/postal order for £ ....

☐ Please send me further details of your work.

Name: ....

Address: ....

....

....

....

Code: N95/3